"Do You Know What An Obsession Is, Meredith?"

Blake asked.

"Yes, I think so."

"Well, that's what I feel for you." He shifted so that he could see her. "Obsessed," he repeated, letting his green-eyed gaze slide over her. "I don't know why. You aren't beautiful. But you arouse me as no other woman ever has or ever will. I don't want anyone but you."

Meredith didn't know if she was still breathing. The admission knocked the wind out of her, took the strength from her legs. She looked at him helplessly.

"You haven't...seen me in five years," she murmured, her heart pounding.

"I've seen you every night," he ground out. "Every time I closed my eyes." He bit back a curse. His eyes were tormented. "I see you in my bed every damned night of my life," he breathed.

"I want you to the point of madness."

Dear Reader:

Happy New Year!

It takes two to tango, and we've declared 1989 as the "Year of the Man" at Silhouette Desire. We're honoring that perfect partner, the magnificent male, the one without whom there would *be* no romance. January marks the beginning of a twelve-month extravaganza spotlighting one book each month as a tribute to the Silhouette Desire hero—our *Man of the Month*!

Created by your favorite authors, you'll find these men are utterly irresistible. You'll be swept away by Diana Palmer's Mr. January (whom some might remember from a brief appearance in *Fit for a King*), and Joan Hohl's Mr. February is every woman's idea of the perfect Valentine....

Don't let these men get away!

Yours,

Isabel Swift
Senior Editor & Editorial Coordinator

DIANA PALMER
Reluctant Father

Silhouette Desire

Published by Silhouette Books New York

America's Publisher of Contemporary Romance

SILHOUETTE BOOKS
300 East 42nd St., New York, N.Y. 10017

ISBN: 0-373-05469-6

First Silhouette Books printing January 1989

Printed in the U.S.A.

DIANA PALMER

writes: "I'm very flattered to lauch Silhouette Desire's year long *Man of the Month* program with 'Mr. January.' I was intrigued with Blake Donovan from the moment he popped up in *Fit for a King*, and I hope you enjoy reading it."

For Margaret, with love

One

Blake Donavan didn't know which was the bigger shock—the dark-haired, unsmiling little girl at his front door or the news that the child was his daughter by his ex-wife.

Blake's pale green eyes darkened dangerously. It had been a hell of a day altogether, and now this. The lawyer who'd just imparted the information stepped closer to the child.

Blake raked his fingers through his unruly black hair and glared down at the child through thick black lashes. His daughter? The scowl grew and his expression hardened, emphasizing the harsh scar down one lean, tanned cheek. He looked even taller and more formidable than he really was.

"I don't like him," the little girl murmured, glaring at Blake as she spoke for the first time. She thrust her lower lip out and moved closer to the lawyer, clinging to his trouser leg. She had green eyes. That fact registered almost immediately—that and her high cheekbones. Blake had high cheekbones, too.

"Now, now." The tall, bespectacled man cleared his throat. "We mustn't be naughty, Sarah."

"My wife," Blake said coldly, "left me five years ago to take up residence with an oilman from Louisiana. I haven't seen or heard from her since."

"If I might come in, Mr. Donavan...?"

He ignored the attorney's plea. "We only cohabited for a month—just long enough for her to find out that I was up to my neck in legal battles. She cut her losses and got out quick with her new lover." He smiled crookedly. "She didn't expect me to win. But I did."

The lawyer glanced around at the elegant, columned front porch, the well-kept gardens, the Mercedes in the driveway. He'd heard about the Donavan fortune and the fight Blake Donavan had when his uncle died and left him fending off numerous greedy cousins.

"The problem, you see," the attorney continued, glancing worriedly at the clinging child, "is that your ex-wife died earlier this month in an airplane crash. Understandably her second husband, from whom she was estranged, didn't want to assume responsibility for the child. Sarah has no one else," he added on a weary sigh. "Your wife's parents were middle-aged when she was born, and she had no brothers or sisters. The entire family is dead. And Sarah is your child."

Blake stared down at the little girl half-angrily. He hadn't even kept a photograph of Nina to remind him of the fool he'd been. And now here was her child, and they expected him to want her.

"I don't have room in my life for a child," he said curtly, furious at the curve fate had thrown him. "She can be put in a home somewhere, I suppose...."

And that was when it happened. The child began to cry. There wasn't a sound from her. She went from belligerence to heartrending sorrow in seconds, with great tears rolling from her green eyes down her flushed round cheeks. The effect was all the more poignant because of her silence and the stoic look on her face, as if she hated giving way to tears in front of the enemy.

Blake felt a stirring inside that surprised him. His mother had died soon after he was born. She hadn't been a particularly moral woman, according to his uncle, and all he knew about her was what little he'd been told. His uncle had taken him in and had adopted him. He, like Sarah, had been an extra person in the world, unwanted by just about everyone. He had no idea who his father was. If it hadn't been for his very wealthy uncle, he wouldn't even have a name. That lack of love and security in his young life had turned him hard. It would turn Sarah hard, too, if she had nobody to protect her.

He looked down at the little girl with a headful of angry questions, hating those tears. But the child had grit. She glared at him and abruptly wiped the tears away with a chubby little hand.

Blake lifted his chin pugnaciously. Already the kid was getting to him. But he wasn't going to be taken in by some scam. He trusted no one. "How do I know she's mine?" he demanded to the lawyer.

"She has your blood type," the man replied. "Your ex-wife's second husband has a totally different blood group. As you know, a blood test can only tell who the father wasn't. It wasn't her second husband."

Blake was about to remark that it could have been any one of a dozen other men, but then he remembered that Nina had married him for what she thought was his soon-to-be-realized wealth. He reasoned that Nina was too

shrewd to have risked losing him by indulging in a fling.
And after she knew what a struggle it was going to be to get
that wealth, she hadn't wanted her newest catch to know
she was already pregnant.

"Why didn't she tell me?" Blake asked coldly.

"She allowed her second husband to think the child was
his," he said quietly. "It wasn't until she died and Sarah's
birth certificate was found that he discovered she was
yours. Nina had apparently decided that Sarah had a right
to her own father's name. By then her second marriage was
already on the rocks, from what I was told." He touched
the child's dark hair absently. "You have the resources to
double-check all this, of course."

"Of course." He stared down his broken nose at the little girl's face. "What's her name again? Sarah?"

"That's right. Sarah Jane."

Blake turned. "Bring her inside. Mrs. Jackson can feed
her and I'll engage a nurse for her."

Just that quickly, he made the decision to keep the child.
But, then, he'd been making quick decisions for a long
time. When his uncle had attempted to link him with
Meredith Calhoun, Blake had quickly decided to marry
Nina. And as a last effort to force Blake into marrying
Meredith, his uncle had left Meredith twenty percent of the
stock in the real-estate conglomerate Blake was to inherit.

That had backfired. Blake had laughed at Meredith, in
front of the whole family gathered for the reading of the
will. And he'd told them all, his arm protectively around
a smiling Nina, that he'd rather lose his inheritance and a
leg than marry a skinny, plain, repulsive woman like Meredith. He was marrying Nina and Meredith could take her
stock and burn it, for all he cared.

His heart lay like lead in his chest as he remembered the
harsh words he'd used that day to cut Meredith down. She

hadn't even flinched, but he'd watched something die in her soft gray eyes. With a kind of ravished dignity, she'd walked out of the room with every eye on her straight back. That had been bad enough. But later she'd come to offer him the stock and he'd been irritated by the faint hunger in her soft eyes. Because she disturbed him, he'd kissed her roughly, bruising her mouth, and he'd said some things that sent her running from him. He regretted that most of all. He planned to marry Nina, but despite his feeling for her, Meredith had been a tiny thorn in his side for years. He hadn't really meant to hurt her. He'd only wanted to make her go away. Well, he had. And he hadn't seen her since. She'd become internationally famous with her women's novels, one of which had been adapted for television. He saw her books everywhere these days. Like Meredith, they haunted him.

It hadn't been until after Nina had left him that he'd found out the reason for Meredith's haste in getting away. She'd been in love with him, his uncle's attorney had told him ruefully as he handed Blake the documents to sign that would give him full control of the Donavan empire. His uncle had known it and had hoped to make Blake see what a good catch she was.

Blake remembered vividly the day he'd discovered his hunger for Meredith. It had shocked them both. His uncle had come into the stable just in time to break up what might have been a disastrous confrontation between them. Blake had lost control and frightened Meredith, although she'd been so sweetly responsive at first that he hadn't seen her fear until the sound of a car driving up had brought him to his senses. Even a blind man couldn't have missed the faint swell of Meredith's mouth, the color in her cheeks and the way she was trembling. That was probably when the old man got the idea about the stock.

What irony, Blake thought, that what he'd wanted most
in life was just a little love. He'd never had his mother's.
He'd never known his father. And his uncle, though fond
of him, was a manipulative man interested in the survival
of his empire through Blake. Blake had actually married
Nina because she'd flattered him and played up to him and
sworn that she loved him. Now, looking back, he could see
that she'd loved his money, not him. Once there was any
possibility of the fortune being lost, she'd walked out on
him. But Meredith had genuinely loved Blake, and he'd
been cruel to her. That had haunted him all these years—
that he'd hurt the one human being on earth who'd ever
wanted to love him.

Meredith's father had worked for Blake's uncle, but the
two men were good friends, as well. Uncle Dan had been
at Meredith's christening as her godfather, and when she'd
grown into her teens and expressed an interest in writing
local history for the school newspaper, Uncle Dan had
opened his library to her and spent hours telling her stories
he'd heard from his grandfather about the old days. Meredith would sit and listen, her big eyes wide, her mouth
faintly smiling. And Blake would brood, because his uncle
had never given him that kind of time and affection. Blake
was useful, but his uncle loved Meredith. He felt as if she'd
usurped the only place in the world he had, and he'd re-
sented her bitterly. And it was more than just that. He'd
already learned that he couldn't trust people. He knew that
Meredith and her parents were dirt poor, and he often
wondered if she might not have some mercenary reason for
hanging around the Donavan house. Too late, he discovered that she hung around because of him. Knowing the
truth put salt in an old wound.

Plain Meredith, with her stringy dark hair and her pale
gray eyes and her heart-shaped face. His uncle had loved

her. Blake had almost despised her, especially after what had happened in the stable when he lost control with her. But under the resentment was an obsessive desire for Meredith that angered him, until it reached flash point the day his uncle's will was read. He'd given his word to Nina that he'd marry her and he couldn't honorably go back on it, but he'd wanted Meredith. God, how he'd wanted her, for years!

She'd loved him, he thought wearily as he led the lawyer and child into the study. Nobody else ever had felt that way about him. His uncle had enjoyed their battles; they'd been friends. His death had been a terrible, unexpected blow, made worse by the fact that he'd always felt that his uncle might have cared for him if Meredith hadn't always been underfoot. Not that it was love that had caused his uncle to adopt him. That had been business.

Maybe his mother would have loved him if she'd lived, although his uncle had described her as a pretty, self-centered woman who simply liked men too much.

So it had come as a shock to find out what shy young Meredith had felt for him. It didn't help to remember how he'd cut her to pieces in public and private. Over the years since she'd left for Texas in the middle of the night on a bus, without a goodbye to anyone, he'd agonized over what he'd done to her. Twice, he'd almost gone to see her when her name started cropping up on book covers. But the past was best left in the past, he'd decided finally. And he had nothing to give her, anyway. Nina had destroyed that part of him that was capable of trust. He had no more to give—to anyone.

He dragged his thoughts away from the past and looked at the child, who was staring plaintively and a little apprehensively at the door, because the lawyer had just smiled and was now making his way out, patent relief written all

over his thin features. Sarah sat very still on the edge of a
blue wing chair, biting her lower lip, her eyes wide and
frightened, although she tried to hide her fear from the
cold, mean-looking man they said was her father.

Blake sat down across from her in his own big red
leather armchair, aware that he looked more like a des-
perado in his jeans and worn chambray shirt than a man
of means. He'd been out in the pasture helping brand cattle, just for the hell of it. At least when he was working
with his hands on the small ranch where he ran purebred
Hereford cattle, he could let his mind go. It beat the hell
out of the trying board meeting he'd had to endure at his
company headquarters in Oklahoma City that morning.

"So you're Sarah," he said. Children made him uncomfortable, and he didn't know how he was going to cope
with this one. But she had his eyes and he couldn't let her
go to strangers. Not if there was one chance in a million
that she really was his daughter.

Sarah lifted her eyes to his, then glanced away, shifting
restlessly. The lawyer had said she was almost four, but she
seemed amazingly mature. She behaved as if she'd never
known the company of other children. It was possible that
she hadn't. He couldn't picture Nina entertaining children. It was totally out of character, but he hadn't realized that when he'd lost his head and married her. Funny
how easy it was to imagine Meredith Calhoun with a lap-
ful of little girls, laughing and playing with them, picking
daisies in the meadow....

He had to stop thinking about Meredith, he told himself firmly. He didn't want her, even if there was a chance
in hell that she'd ever come back to Jack's Corner, Oklahoma. And he knew without a doubt that she certainly
didn't want him.

"I don't like you," Sarah said after a minute. She shifted in the chair and glanced around her. "I don't want to live here." She glared at Blake.

He glared back. "Well, I'm not crazy about the idea, either, but it looks like we're stuck with each other."

Her lower lip jutted, and for an instant she looked just like him. "I'll bet you don't even have a cat."

"God forbid," he grumbled. "I hate cats."

She sighed and looked at her scuffed shoes with something like resignation and a patience far beyond her years. She appeared tired and worn. "My mommy isn't coming back." She pulled at her dress. "She didn't like me. You don't like me, either," she said, lifting her chin. "I don't care. You're not really my daddy."

"I must be." He sighed heavily. "God knows, you look enough like me."

"You're ugly."

His eyebrows shot up. "You're no petunia yourself, sprout," he returned.

"The ugly duckling turns into a swan," she told him with a faraway look in her eyes.

She twirled her hands in her dress. He noticed then, for the first time, that it was old. The lace was stained and the dress was rumpled. He frowned.

"Where have you been staying?" he asked her.

"Mommy left me with Daddy Brad, but he had to go out a lot, so Mrs. Smathers took care of me." She looked up, and the expression in her green eyes was old for a little girl's. "Mrs. Smathers says that children are horrible," she said dramatically, "and that they belong in cages. I cried when Mommy left, and she locked me up and said she'd leave me there if I didn't hush." Her lower lip trembled, but she didn't cry. "I got out, too, and ran away." She shrugged. "But nobody came to find me, so I went home.

Mrs. Smathers was real mad, but Daddy Brad didn't care. He said I wasn't his real child and it didn't matter if I ran away.''

Blake could imagine that ''Daddy Brad'' was upset to find that the child he'd accepted as his own was somebody else's, but taking it out on the child seemed pretty callous.

He leaned back in his chair, wondering what in hell he was going to do with his short houseguest. He didn't know anything about kids. He wasn't sure he even liked them. And this one already looked like a handful. She was outspoken and belligerent and not much to look at. He could see trouble ahead.

Mrs. Jackson came into the room to see if Blake wanted anything, and stopped dead. She was fifty-five, a spinster, graying and thin and faintly intimidating to people who didn't know her. She was used to a bachelor household, and the sight of a child sitting across from her boss was vaguely unnerving.

''Who's that?'' she asked, without dressing up the question.

Sarah looked at her and sighed, as if saying, oh, no, here's another sour one. Blake almost laughed out loud at the expression on the child's face.

''This is Amie Jackson, Sarah,'' Blake said, introducing them. ''Mrs. Jackson, Sarah Jane is my daughter.''

Mrs. Jackson didn't faint, but she did go a shade redder. ''Yes, sir, that's hard to miss,'' she said, comparing the small, composed child's face with its older male counterpart. ''Her mother isn't here?'' she added, staring around as if she expected Nina to materialize.

''Nina is dead,'' Blake said without any particular feeling. Nina had knocked the finer feelings out of him years ago. His own foolish blindness to her real nature had helped her in the task.

"Oh, I'm sorry." Mrs. Jackson rubbed her apron between her thin hands for something to do. "Would she like some milk and cookies?" she asked hesitantly.

"That might be nice. Sarah?" Blake asked more curtly than he'd meant.

Sarah shifted and stared at the carpet. "I'd get crumbs on the floor." She shook her head. "Mrs. Smathers says kids should eat off the kitchen floor 'cause they're messy."

Mrs. Jackson looked uncomfortable, and Blake sighed heavily. "You can get crumbs on the floor. Nobody's going to yell at you."

Sarah glanced up hesitantly.

"I don't mind cleaning up crumbs," Mrs. Jackson said testily. "Do you want cookies?"

"Yes, please."

The older woman nodded curtly and went to get some.

"Nobody smiles here," Sarah murmured. "It's just like home."

Blake felt a twinge of regret for the child, who seemed to have been stuck away in the housekeeper's corner with no thought for her well-being. And not just since her stepfather had found out that she was Blake's child, apparently.

His eyes narrowed and he asked the question that was consuming him. "Didn't your mother stay with you?"

"Mommy was busy," Sarah said. "She said I had to stay with Mrs. Smathers and do what she said."

"Wasn't she home from time to time?"

"She and my daddy—" she faltered and grimaced "—my *other* daddy yelled at each other mostly. Then she went away and he went away, too."

This was getting them nowhere. He stood and began to pace, his hands in his pockets, his face stormy and hard.

Sarah watched him covertly. "You sure are big," she murmured.

He stopped, glancing down at her curiously. "You sure are little," he returned.

"I'll grow," Sarah promised. "Do you have a horse?"

"Several."

She brightened. "I can ride a horse!"

"Not on my ranch, you can't."

Her green eyes flashed fire. "I can so if I want to. I can ride any horse!"

He knelt in front of her very slowly, and his green eyes met hers levelly and without blinking. "No," he said firmly. "You'll do what you're told, and you won't talk back. This is my place, and I make the rules. Got it?"

She hesitated, but only for a minute. "Okay," she said sulkily.

He touched the tip of her pert nose. "And no sulking. I don't know how this is going to work out," he added curtly. "Hell, I don't know anything about kids!"

"Hell is where you go when you're bad," Sarah replied matter-of-factly. "My mommy's friend used to talk about it all the time, and about damns and sons of—"

"Sarah!" Blake burst out, shocked that a child her age should be so familiar with bad words.

"Do you have any cows?" she added, easily diverted.

"A few," he muttered. "Which one of your mummy's friends used language like that around you?"

"Just Trudy," she said, wide-eyed.

Blake whistled through his teeth and turned just as Mrs. Jackson came in with a tray of milk and cookies for Sarah and coffee for Blake.

"I like coffee," Sarah said. "My mommy let me drink it when she had hers in bed and she wasn't awake good."

"I'll bet," Blake said, "but you aren't drinking it here. Coffee isn't good for kids."

"I can have coffee if I want to," Sarah returned belligerently.

Blake looked at Mrs. Jackson, who was more or less frozen in place, staring at the little girl as she grabbed four cookies and proceeded to stuff them into her mouth as if she hadn't eaten in days.

"You quit, or even try to quit," Blake told the housekeeper, who'd looked after his uncle before him, "and so help me God, I'll track you all the way to Alaska and drag you back here by one foot."

"Me, quit? Just when things are getting interesting?" Mrs. Jackson lifted her chin. "God forbid."

"Sarah, when was the last time you ate?" Blake inquired, watching her grab another handful of cookies.

"I had supper," she said, "and then we came here."

"You haven't had breakfast?" he burst out. "Or lunch?"

She shook her head. "These cookies are good!"

"If you haven't eaten for almost a day, I imagine so." He sighed. "You'd better make us an early dinner tonight," Blake told Mrs. Jackson. "She'll eat herself sick on cookies if we're not careful."

"Yes, sir. I'll go and make up the guest room for her," she said. "But what about clothes? Does she have a suitcase?"

"No, that lawyer didn't bring anything. Let her sleep in her slip tonight. Tomorrow," he added, "you can take her into town to do some shopping."

"Me?" Mrs. Jackson looked horrified.

"Somebody has to be sacrificed," he told her pithily. "And I'm the boss."

Mrs. Jackson's lips formed a thin line. "I don't know beans about little girls' clothes!"

"Well, take her to Mrs. Donaldson's shop," he muttered. "That's where King Roper and Elissa take their little girl to be outfitted. I heard King groan about the prices, but that won't bother us any more than it bothers them."

"Yes, sir." She turned to leave.

"By the way, where's the weekly paper?" he asked, because it always came on Thursday morning. "I wanted to see if our legal ad got in."

Mrs. Jackson shifted uncomfortably and grimaced. "Well, I didn't want to upset you..."

His eyebrows arched. "How could the weekly paper possibly upset me? Get it!"

"All right. If you're sure that's what you want." She reached into the drawer of one of the end tables and pulled it out. "There you go, boss. And I'll leave before the explosion, if you don't mind."

She exited, and Sarah took two more cookies while Blake stared down at the paper's front page at a face that had haunted him.

"Author Meredith Calhoun to autograph at Baker's Book Nook," read the headline, and underneath it was a recent picture of Meredith.

His eyes searched over it in shock. The plain, skinny woman he'd hurt bore no resemblance to this peacock. Her brown hair was pulled back from her face into an elegant chignon. Her gray eyes were serene in a high-cheekboned face that could have graced the cover of a magazine, and her makeup enhanced the raw material that had always been there. She was wearing a pale suit coat with a pastel blouse, and she looked lovely. More than lovely. She looked soft and warm and totally untouched at the age of twenty-five, which she had to be now.

Blake put the paper down after scanning what he already knew about her skyrocketing career and her latest book, *Choices*, about a man and a woman trying to manage careers, marriage and parenthood all at once. He'd read it, as he secretly read all Meredith's books, looking for traces of the past. Maybe even for a cessation of hostilities. But her feelings for him were buried and there was never a single trait he could recognize in her people that reminded him of himself. It was as if she sensed that he might look at them and had hidden anything that would give her inner feelings away.

Sarah Jane was standing beside him without his knowing it. She looked at the picture in the paper. "That's a pretty lady," Sarah said. She leaned forward and picked out a word in the column below the photograph. "*B...o...o...k*. Book," she said proudly.

"So it is." He pointed to the name. "How about that?"

"*M...e...r*...Merry Christmas," she said.

He smiled faintly. "Meredith," he corrected. "That's her name. She's a writer."

"I had a book about the three bears," Sarah told him. "Did she write that?"

"No. She writes books for big girls. Finish your cookies and you can watch television."

"I like to watch *Mr. Rogers* and *Sesame Street*," she said.

He frowned. "What?"

"They come on television."

"Oh. Well, help yourself."

He moved out of the room, ignoring the coffee. Which was sad, because Sarah Jane discovered it in the big silver pot and proceeded to help herself to the now cool liquid while he was on the telephone in the hall. Her cry caused him to drop the receiver in mid-sentence.

She was drenched in coffee and screaming her head off. She wasn't the only wet thing, either. The carpet and part of the sofa were saturated and the tray was an inch deep with black liquid.

"I told you to stay out of the coffee, didn't I?" Blake said as he knelt to see if she had been burned. Which, thank God, she hadn't; she was more frightened than hurt.

"I wanted some," she murmured tearfully. "I ruined my pretty dress."

"That isn't all that's going to get ruined, either," he said ominously, and abruptly tugged her over his knee and gave her bottom a slap. "When I say no, I mean no. Do you understand me, Sarah Jane Donavan?" he asked firmly.

She was too surprised to cry anymore. She stared at him warily. "Is that my name now?"

"It's always been your name," he replied. "You're a Donavan. This is your home."

"I like coffee," she said hesitantly.

"And I said you weren't to drink it," he reminded her.

She took a deep breath. "Okay." She picked up the coffeepot, only to have it taken from her and put on the table. "I can clean it up," she said. "Mommy always made me clean up my mess."

"This is more than you can cope with, sprout. And God only knows what we're going to put on you while those things are washed."

Mrs. Jackson came in and put both hands to her mouth. "Saints alive!"

"Towels, quick," Blake said.

She went to get them, muttering all the way.

Minutes later the mess was gone, Sarah Jane was bundled up in a makeshift towel dress and her clothes were being washed and dried. Blake went into his study and locked the door, shamelessly leaving Mrs. Jackson to cope with Sarah while he had a few minutes' peace. He had a feeling that it was going to be more and more difficult to find any quiet place in his life from now on.

He wasn't sure he was going to like being a father. It was a whole new kind of responsibility, and his daughter seemed to have inherited his strength of will and stubbornness. She was going to be a handful. Mrs. Jackson knew no more about kids than he did, and that wasn't going to help, either. But he didn't feel right about sending Sarah off to a boarding school. He knew what it was like to be alone and unwanted and not too physically appealing. He felt a kind of kinship with this child, and he was reluctant to push her out of his life. On the other hand, how in hell was he going to live with her?

But over and above that problem was the newest one. Meredith Calhoun was coming to Jack's Corner for a whole month, according to that newspaper. In that length of time he was sure to see her, and he had mixed feelings about opening up the old wounds. He wondered if she felt the same way, or if, in her fame and wealth, she'd left the memories of him in the past. He wanted to see her all the same. Even if she still hated him.

Two

Blake and Mrs. Jackson usually ate their evening meal with a minimum of conversation. But that was another old custom that was going to change.

Sarah Jane was a walking encyclopedia of questions. One answer led to another why and another, until Blake was ready to get under the table. And just the mention of bedtime brought on a tantrum. Mrs. Jackson tried to cajole the child into obeying, but Sarah Jane only got louder. Blake settled the matter by picking her up and carrying her to her new room.

Mrs. Jackson helped her undress and get into bed and Blake paused at her bedside reluctantly to say good-night.

"You don't like me," Sarah accused.

He almost bristled at her mutinous expression, but she was a proud child, and he didn't want to break her spirit. She'd need it as she grew older.

"I don't know you," he replied reasonably. "Any more than you know me. People don't become friends on the spur of the moment. It takes time, sprout."

She considered that as she lay there, swallowed whole by the size of the bed under her and the thick white coverlet over her. She watched him curiously. "You don't hate little children, do you?" she asked finally.

"I don't hate kids," he said. "I'm just not used to them. I've been by myself for a long time."

"Did you love my mommy?"

That question was harder to answer. His broad shoulders rose and fell. "I thought she was beautiful. I wanted to marry her."

"She didn't like me," Sarah confided. "Can I really stay here? And I don't have to go back to Daddy Brad?"

"No, you don't have to go back. We'll have to do some adjusting, Sarah, but we'll get used to each other."

"I'm scared with the light off," she confessed.

"We'll leave a night-light on."

"What if a monster comes?" she asked.

"I'll kill it, of course," he reassured her with a smile.

She shifted under the covers. "Aren't you scared of monsters?"

"Nope."

She smiled for the first time. "Okay." She stared at him for a minute. "You have a scar on your face," she said, pointing to his right cheek.

His fingers touched it absently. "So I do." He'd long ago given up being sensitive about it, but he didn't like going into the way he'd gotten it. "Good night, sprout."

He didn't offer to read her a story or tell her one. In fact, he didn't know any he could tell a child. And he didn't tuck her in or kiss her. That would have been awkward. But Sarah didn't ask for those things or seem to need them.

Perhaps she hadn't had much affection. She acted very much like a child who'd been turned loose and not bothered with overmuch.

He went back downstairs and into his study, to finish the day's business that had been put on hold while he'd coped with Sarah's arrival. Tomorrow Mrs. Jackson would have to handle things. He couldn't steal time from a board meeting for one small child.

Jack's Corner was a medium-sized Oklahoma city, and Blake's office was in a new mall complex that was both modern and spacious. The next day, he and his board were just finalizing the financing for an upcoming project, when his secretary came in, flustered and apprehensive.

"Mr. Donavan, it's your housekeeper on the phone. Could you speak with her, please?"

"I told you not to interrupt me unless it was urgent, Daisy," he told the young blond woman curtly.

She hesitated nervously. "Please, sir?"

He got up and excused himself, striding angrily out into the waiting room to pick up the phone with a hard glare at Daisy.

"Okay, Amie, what's wrong?" he asked shortly.

"I quit."

"Oh, my God, not yet," he shot back. "Not until she starts dating, at least!"

"I can't wait that long, and I want my check today," Mrs. Jackson snorted.

"Why?"

She held out the receiver. "Do you hear that?"

He did. Sarah Jane was screaming her head off.

"Where are you?" he asked with cold patience.

"Meg Donaldson's dress shop downtown," she replied. "This has been going on for five minutes. I wouldn't let her buy the dress she wanted and I can't make her stop."

"Smack her on the bottom," Blake said.

"Hit her in public?" She sounded as if he'd asked her to tie the child to a moving vehicle by her hair. "I won't!"

He said something under his breath. "All right, I'm on my way."

He hung up. "Tell the board to go ahead without me," he told Daisy shortly, grabbing his hat off the hat rack. "I have to go administrate a small problem."

"When will you be back, sir?" Daisy asked.

"God knows."

He closed the door behind him with a jerk, mentally consigning fatherhood and sissy housekeepers to the netherworld.

It took him ten minutes to get to the small children's boutique in town, and as luck would have it, there was one empty space in front that he could slide the Mercedes into. Next to his car was a sporty red Porsche with the top down. He paused for a moment to admire it and wonder about the owner.

"Oh, thank God." Mrs. Jackson almost fell on him when he walked into the shop. "Make her stop."

Sarah was lying on the floor, her face red and tear stained, her hair damp with sweat, her old dress rumpled from her exertions. She looked up at Blake and the tantrum died abruptly. "She won't buy me the frilly one," she moaned, pouting with a demure femininity.

My God, Blake thought absently, they learn how to do it almost before they can walk.

"Why won't you buy her the frilly one?" he asked an astonished Mrs. Jackson, the words slipping out before he could stop them, while Meg Donaldson smothered a smile behind her cupped hands at the counter.

Mrs. Jackson looked taken aback. She cleared her throat. "Well, it's expensive."

"I'm rich," he pointed out.

"Yes, but it's not suitable for playing in the backyard. She needs some jeans and tops and underthings."

"I need a dress to wear to parties," Sarah sobbed. "I never got to go to a party, but you can have one for me, and I can make friends."

He reached down and lifted her to her feet, then knelt in front of her. "I don't like tantrums," he said. "Next time Mrs. Jackson will spank you. In public," he added, glaring at the stoic housekeeper.

She turned beet red, and Mrs. Donaldson bent down beside the counter as if she were going to look for something and burst out laughing.

While Mrs. Jackson was searching for words, the shop door opened and two women came in. Elissa Roper was immediately recognizable. She was married to King Roper, a friend of Blake's.

"Blake!" Elissa smiled. "We haven't seen you lately. What are you and Mrs. Jackson doing in here? And who's this?"

"This is my daughter, Sarah Jane," Blake said, introducing the child. "We've just been having a tantrum."

"Speak for yourself," Mrs. Jackson sniffed. "I don't have tantrums. I just resign from jobs that have gotten too big for me."

"You're resigning, Mrs. Jackson? That would be one for the books, wouldn't it?" a soft, amused voice asked, and Blake's heart jumped.

He got slowly to his feet, oblivious to Sarah's curious stare, to come face to face with a memory.

Meredith Calhoun looked back at him with gray eyes that gave away nothing except faint humor. She was wearing a blue dress with a white jacket, and she looked expensive and sophisticated and lovely. Her figure had filled out over the years, and she was tall and exquisite, with full, high breasts and a narrow waist flaring to hips that were in exact proportion for her body. She had long legs encased in silk hose, and elegant feet in white sandals. And the sight of her made Blake ache in the most inconvenient way.

"Merry!" Mrs. Jackson enthused, and hugged her. "It's been so long!"

And it had been since Mrs. Jackson had made cake and cookies for her while she visited Blake's uncle, who was also her godfather.

She and the housekeeper had grown close. "Long enough, I guess, Amie," Meredith said as they stepped apart. "You haven't aged a day."

"You have," Mrs. Jackson said with a smile. "You're grown up."

"And famous," Elissa put in. "Bess—you remember my sister-in-law—and Meredith were in the same class at school and are still great friends. She's staying with Bess and Bobby."

"They've just bought the house next door to me," Blake replied, for something to say. He couldn't find the words to express what he felt when he looked at Meredith. So many years, so much pain. But whatever she'd felt for him was gone. That fact registered immediately.

"Has Nina come back with your daughter?" Elissa asked, trying not to appear poleaxed, which she was.

"Nina died earlier this year. Sarah Jane is living with me now." He dragged his eyes away from Meredith to turn his attention to his child. "You look terrible. Go to the rest room and wash your face."

"You come, too," Sarah said mutinously.

"No."

"I won't go!"

"I'll take her," Mrs. Jackson said in her best martyred tone.

"No! You won't let me buy the frilly dress!" Sarah turned her attention to the two curious onlookers. "She's in the paper," she said, her eyes on Meredith. "She writes books. My daddy said so."

Meredith managed not to look at Blake. The unexpected sight of him after so much time was enough to knock her speechless. Thank God she'd learned to mask her emotions and hadn't given herself away. The last thing she wanted to do was let Blake Donavan see that she had any vulnerability left.

Sarah walked over to Meredith, staring up at her with rapt fascination. "Can you tell stories?"

"Oh, I guess I can," she said, smiling at the child who was so much like Blake. "You've got red eyes, Sarah. You shouldn't cry."

"I want the frilly dress and a party and other little children to play with. It's very lonely, and they don't like me." She indicated Blake and Mrs. Jackson.

"One day, and she's advertising to the world that we're Jekyll and Hyde." Mrs. Jackson threw up her hands.

"Which one are you?" Blake returned, glaring at her.

"Jekyll, of course. I'm prettier than you are," Mrs. Jackson shot back.

"Just like old times," Elissa said with a sigh, "isn't it, Merry?"

Meredith wasn't listening. Sarah Jane had reached up and taken her hand.

"You can come with me," the little girl told Meredith. "I like her," she said to her father belligerently. "She smiles. I'll let her wash my face."

"Do you mind?" Blake asked Meredith, speaking to her for the first time since she'd entered the shop.

"I don't mind." She didn't look at him fully, then turned and let Sarah lead her into the small bathroom in the back of the shop.

"She's changed," Mrs. Jackson said to Mrs. Donaldson. "I hardly knew her."

"It's been a long time, you know. And she's a famous woman now, not the child who left us."

Blake walked away uncomfortably, staring at the dresses. Elissa moved closer to him while the other two women talked. She'd been a little afraid of Blake when she'd first met him years ago, but she'd gotten to know him better. He and King were friends and visited regularly.

"How long has Sarah been with you?" she asked him.

"Since yesterday afternoon," he replied dryly. "It seems like years. I guess I'll get used to her, but it's hard going right now. She's a handful."

"She's just frightened and alone," Elissa replied. "She'll improve when she has time to settle down and adjust."

"I may be bankrupt by then," he mused. "I had to walk out of a board meeting. And all because Sarah Jane wanted a frilly dress."

"Why don't you buy it for her and she can come to my Danielle's birthday party next week? It will be nice for her to meet children her own age."

"She'll sit on the cake and wreck the house," he groaned.

"No, she won't. She's just a little girl."

"She wrecked my living room in just under ten minutes," he assured her.

"It takes mine five minutes to do that." Elissa grinned. "It's normal."

He stared toward the bathroom. Meredith and Sarah Jane were just coming out. "There are people in the world who have more than one," he murmured. "Do you suppose they're sane?"

Elissa laughed. "Yes. You'll understand it all one day."

"Look what Merry gave me!" Sarah enthused, showing Blake a snowy white handkerchief. "And it's all mine! It has lace!"

Blake shook his head as she turned abruptly and grabbed the dress she'd been screaming about. "It's mine. I want it. Oh, please." She changed tactics, staring up pie eyed at her daddy. "It will go so nicely with my new handkerchief."

Blake laughed and then caught himself. He looked at Mrs. Jackson. "What do you think?"

"I think that if you buy Sarah Jane that dress I'm going to put it on you," the older woman replied in a hunted tone.

"You really shouldn't give in because children have tantrums, Blake," Mrs. Donaldson volunteered. "I know. I raised four."

He stared at Mrs. Jackson. "You started this. Why would you tell her she couldn't have the damned thing in the first place?"

"I told you, it was too expensive for her to play in."

"She'll need a dress to come to Danielle's party," Elissa broke in.

"Now see what you've done," Blake growled at Mrs. Jackson.

"I won't take her shopping ever again. You can just let somebody else run your company and do it yourself," Mrs. Jackson grumbled.

"I don't know what to think of a woman who can't manage to buy a dress for one small child."

"That isn't just one small child, that's one small Donavan, and nobody could say she isn't your daughter!" Mrs. Jackson said.

Blake felt an unexpected surge of pleasure at the words. He looked down at the child who looked so much like him and had to agree that she did have some of his better qualities. Stubborn determination. Not to mention good taste.

"You can have the dress, Sarah," he told her, and was rewarded by a smile so delightful he'd have sold his Mercedes to buy the damned thing for her no matter what it cost.

"Oh, thank you!" Sarah gushed.

"You'll be sorry," Mrs. Jackson said.

"You can shut up," he told her. "It's your fault."

"You said to take her shopping, you didn't say what to buy," she reminded him huffily. "And I'm going home."

"Then go on. And don't burn lunch," he called after her.

"I couldn't burn a bologna sandwich if I tried, and that's all you'll get from me today!"

"I'll fire you!"

"Thank God!"

Blake glared at Mrs. Donaldson and Elissa, who were trying not to smile. This byplay between Blake and Mrs. Jackson was old hat to them, and they found it amusing. Meredith's expression was less revealing. She was looking at Sarah and Blake wished he could see her eyes.

But she turned away. "We'd better get on," she told Elissa. "Bess will be waiting for us to pick her up at the beauty parlor."

"Okay," Elissa grinned. "Just let me get those socks for Danielle and I'll be ready."

She did, which left Meredith stranded with Blake and his daughter.

"Isn't it pretty?" Sarah sighed, pirouetting with the dress held in front of her. "I look like a fairy princess."

"Not quite," Blake said. "You'll need shoes, and some clothes to play in, too."

"Okay." She ran to the other racks and started looking through them.

"Is it normal for them to be so clothes conscious at this age?" Blake asked, turning his attention to Meredith.

"I don't know," she said uncomfortably. His unblinking green-eyed gaze was making her remember too much pain. "I haven't been around children very much. I must go...."

He touched her arm, and was astonished to find that she jerked away from his touch and stared fully at him with eyes that burned with resentment and pain and anger.

"So, you haven't forgotten," he said under his breath.

"Did you really think I ever would?" she asked on a shaky laugh. "You were the reason I never came back here. I almost didn't come this time, either, but I was tired of hiding."

He didn't know what to say. Her reaction was unexpected. He'd imagined that she might have some bitterness, but not this much. He searched what he could see of her face, looking for something he knew he wasn't going to find anymore.

"You've changed," he said quietly.

Her eyes looked up into his, and there was a flash of cold anger there. "Oh, yes, I've changed. I've grown up. That should reassure you. I won't be chasing after you like a lovesick puppy this time."

The reference stung, and she'd meant it to. He'd accused her of chasing him and more, after the reading of the will.

But being reminded of the past only made him bitter, and he hit back. "Thank God," he said with a mocking smile. "Could I have that in writing?"

"Go to hell," she said under her breath.

That, coming from shy little Meredith, floored him. He didn't even have a comeback.

Sarah came running up with an armload of things. "Look, aren't they pretty! Can I have them all?" she asked the scowling man beside Meredith.

"Sure," he said absently.

Meredith turned away from him, smiling. It was the first time in memory that she'd ever fought back—or for that matter, said anything to him that wasn't respectful and worshipful. What a delightful surprise to find he no longer intimidated her.

"Ready to go?" Meredith asked Elissa.

"Sure am. See you, Blake!"

"But you can't go." Sarah ran to Meredith and caught her skirt. "You're my friend."

The child couldn't know how that hurt—to have Blake's child, the child she might have borne him, cling to her. She knelt in front of Sarah, disengaging the small hand. "I have to go now. But I'll see you again, Sarah. Okay?"

Sarah looked lost. "You're nice. Nobody else smiles at me."

"Mrs. Jackson will smile at you tonight, I promise," Blake told the child. "Or she'll never smile again," he added under his breath.

"You don't smile," Sarah accused him.

"My face would break," he assured her. "Now get your things and we'll go home."

She sighed. "Okay." She looked up at Meredith. "Will you come to see me?"

Meredith went white. Go into that house again, where Blake had humiliated and hurt her? God forbid!

"You can come to see Danielle, Sarah," Elissa interrupted, and Meredith knew then that Elissa had heard the whole story from King. She was running interference, bless her.

"Who's Dan—Danielle?" Sarah asked.

"My daughter. She's four."

"I'm almost four," Sarah said. "Can she say nursery rhymes? I know all of them. 'Humpty Dumpty sat on the wall, Humpty Dumpty—'"

"I'll give your Daddy a call and he can bring you down to Bess's house, where Meredith is staying. Bess is my sister-in-law, and Danielle and I go to see her sometimes."

"I'd like to have a friend," Sarah agreed. "Could we do that?" she asked her father.

Blake was watching Meredith shift uncomfortably. "Sure we can," he said, just to irritate her.

Meredith turned away, her heart going like an overwound watch, her eyes restless and frightened. The very last thing she wanted was to have to cope with Blake.

"Bye, Merry!" Sarah called.

"Goodbye, Sarah Jane," she murmured, and forced a smile, but she wouldn't look at Blake.

He said the appropriate things as Elissa followed Meredith out the door, but the fact that Meredith wouldn't look at him cut like a knife.

He watched Meredith climb in under the wheel of the red Porsche. It didn't seem like the kind of car she'd drive, but she wasn't the girl she'd been. His eyes narrowed. He wondered if she was still as innocent as before, or if some man had taught her all the sweet ways to make love. His face hardened at the thought. No one had touched her until he had. But he'd been rough and he'd frightened her.

He hadn't really meant to. The feel and taste of her had knocked him off balance, and at the time he hadn't been experienced himself. Nina had been his first woman, but his first real intimacy, even if it had been relatively chaste, had been with Meredith. Even after all the years in between, he could feel her mouth, taste its sweetness. He could see the soft alabaster of her breasts when he'd unbuttoned the top of her dress. He groaned silently. That was when he'd lost his senses—seeing her like that. He wondered if she knew how green he'd been in those days, and decided that she was too inexperienced herself to realize it. He'd wanted Meredith to the point of madness, and things had just gotten out of hand. But to a shy young virgin, his ardor must have seemed frightening.

He turned back to his daughter with memories of the past darkening his eyes. It seemed so long ago that the rain had found him in the stable and Meredith had come in looking for his uncle. . . .

Three

It had been late spring that day five years ago, and Blake had been helping one of the men doctor a sick horse in the stable. Meredith had come along just in time to see the second man leave. Blake was still there. She'd come to ask where his uncle was, but it was a rainy day, and she and Blake had been caught in the barn while it stormed outside.

Blake had hungrily watched Meredith as she stood on her tiptoes to look toward the house. She was wearing a white sundress that buttoned up the front, and as she stretched, every line of her body had been emphasized and her dress had ridden up, displaying most of her long legs.

The sight of those slim, elegant legs and the sensuous curve of her body had caught him in the stomach like a body blow, and he'd stood there staring. It shouldn't have affected him. He had Nina, who was blond and beautiful and who loved him. Meredith was plain and shy and not at all the kind of woman who could attract him. But as he'd looked at her, his body had quickened and the shock of it had moved him helplessly toward where she stood in the wide doorway, just out of the path of the rain.

Meredith had heard him, or perhaps sensed him, because she turned, her eyes faintly covetous before she lowered them. "It's really coming down, isn't it?" she asked hesitantly. "I was just about to go home, but I needed to ask your Uncle Dan some more questions."

"You're always around these days," he'd remarked, half-angry because his body was playing cruel tricks on him.

She'd blushed. "He's helping me with some articles for the school paper, and I'm going to do a book with the same information," she'd begun.

"Book!" He scoffed at that. "You're barely twenty. What makes you think you've learned enough to write books? You haven't even started to live."

Her head came up and there had been a flash of anger in her pale gray eyes, which was instantly disguised. "You make me sound like a toddler."

"You look like one occasionally," he remarked with faint humor, noting the braid of her hair, which she'd tied with a ribbon. "And I'm almost twelve years older than you are." He pushed away from the barn door, noticing the faint hunger in her face as he went toward her.

The hunger was what touched him. It hadn't occurred to him that women besides Nina might find him physically attractive. He had that damned scar down one cheek, thanks to Meredith, and it made him look like a renegade. His arrogance didn't soften the impression.

He looked down his nose at Meredith when he was less than a foot from her, watching the expressions play across her face. It was a pretty good bet that she was innocent, and if she'd been kissed, probably it hadn't been often or seriously. That, at least, made him feel confident. She didn't have anyone to compare him with.

His eyes went to her soft bow of a mouth, and with an impulse he didn't even understand at the time, he tilted her chin up with a lean hand and bent to brush his lips over hers.

"Blake...!" she gasped.

He hadn't known if it was fear or shock...hadn't cared. The first contact with her mouth had caused a frightening surge of desire in his lean body. "Don't back away now," he bit off against her soft lips. "Come here."

He'd pulled her against him and his mouth had grown rough and hungry. Even now, five years later, he could feel the soft yielding of her body in his arms, smell the scent of her as she strained upward and gave him her mouth with such warm eagerness. He could hear the rain beating on the stable roof, and the soft sounds of a cow settling down in the darkness beyond where they stood silhouetted against the driving rain.

Blake had been amazed by the tentative response he got from her lips. That shy nibbling drove him over the edge. He eased her back against the wall of the barn, out of sight, with his mouth still covering hers. Then he let his body slide down against her so that his hips were pressing feverishly against hers, his chest crushing her soft young breasts.

He felt her quickened breathing, heard the soft "no!" as he felt for and found one firm breast and touched it through her clothing. The feel of her made him wild. He remembered the white-hot flames that had consumed him with the intimate touch. He'd wanted her with a shuddering passion and his mouth had grown more and more demanding. She gave in to him all at once, her body relaxing, shivering, her mouth shyly responding. His tongue pushed gently inside her lips and she stiffened, but she didn't try to pull away.

Confident now, his fingers worked at buttons and he lifted his head just fractionally to look down at what they uncovered. Her breasts were bare under the dress and he groaned as he bent to brush his mouth against them. He felt her gasp and her hands gripped his arms hard. The silky taste of her body stripped him of control entirely, the feel of her skin against his face made him wild. His hands grew roughly intimate in passion and his mouth closed hungrily over one firm breast.

What might have happened then was anyone's guess. He hardly heard Meredith's frantic voice. It wasn't until he caught the sound of a car driving up that his sanity returned.

He lifted his head, breathing fiercely, in time to see Meredith's eyes full of fear. He realized belatedly what he'd done. He took a sharp breath and levered himself back up, away from her, his body in torment with unsatisfied desire, his eyes smoldering as they met hers.

She blushed furiously as she fumbled buttons into buttonholes, making herself decent again. And only then did he realize how intimate the embrace had gotten. He didn't know what had possessed him. He'd frightened her and himself, because it was the first time he'd ever lost control like that. But, then, he hadn't been experienced, he realized now. Not until he and Nina were married. His first taste of sensual pleasure had been with Meredith that day in the stable.

He didn't speak—he was too shocked. The sudden arrival of his uncle had been a godsend at the time, but later it dawned on him that his uncle had guessed what had happened between Blake and Meredith and had altered his

will to capitalize on it. His favorite godchild and his
nephew—he would have considered them a perfect match.
But Blake hadn't thought of it at the time. He'd been so
drunk on Meredith's soft mouth that he'd almost gone
after her when she mumbled some excuse and ran out into
the rain as he and his uncle watched her.

Then, within days, his uncle was dead of a heart attack.
Blake had been crushed. The sense of loneliness he felt
when it happened was almost too great for words. Meredith had been around, with her parents, but he'd hardly
noticed with Nina clinging to him, pretending sympathy.
And then, suddenly they were reading the will. Blake was
engaged to Nina, but still trying to cope with the turbu-
lent emotions Meredith had aroused in him. The will was
read, and he learned that Uncle Dan had left twenty percent of the stock in his real estate companies to Meredith.
The only way Blake could have it would be by marrying
her.

He had forty-nine percent of the stock, but his cousins
had thirty-one shares between them. And although one of
the cousins down in Texas would have sided with him in a
proxy fight if Meredith sided against him, he could lose
everything. Nina had laughed. He still remembered the
look on her face as she scrutinized Meredith in a manner
too contemptuous for words.

Blake had done much worse. The realization that his
uncle had tried to control his life even from the grave and
the embarrassment of having his haughty cousins snicker
at him was just too much.

"Marry her?" he'd said slowly after the will had been
read, rising out of his chair to confront Meredith in the
dead silence that followed. "My God, marry that plain,
dull, shadow of a woman? I'd rather lose the real estate
companies, the money and my left leg than marry her!"

He'd moved closer to Meredith, watching her cringe and go pale at the humiliation of having him say those things so loudly in front of the family. "No dice, Meredith," he said with venom. "Take the stock and go to hell with it. I don't want you!"

He'd expected her to burst into tears and run out of the room, but she hadn't. Deathly pale, shaking so hard she could barely stand, she lowered her eyes, turned away and walked out with dignity far beyond her twenty years. It had shamed him later to remember her stiff pride and his own loss of control that had prompted the outburst. The cousin from Texas had glared at him with black eyes and walked out without another word, leaving him alone with Nina and the other cousins, who subsequently filed suit to take control of the real estate companies from him.

But Nina had smiled and clung to him and promised heaven, because she was sure he'd get the stock back somehow. She'd advised him to talk to the lawyer.

He had. But the only way to get the stock back, apparently, was to marry Meredith or break the will. Both were equally impossible.

He was still smoldering when he found Meredith coming out the back door. She'd been in the kitchen saying goodbye to Mrs. Jackson.

She was pale and unusually quiet, and she looked as if she didn't want to stop. But he'd gotten in front of her in the deserted, shaded backyard and refused to let her pass.

"I don't want the shares," she said, without looking at him. "I never did. I knew nothing about what your uncle had planned, and I wouldn't have gone through with it if I had."

"Wouldn't you?" he demanded coldly. "Maybe you saw a chance to marry a rich man. Your family is poor."

"There are worse things than being poor," she replied quietly. "And people who marry for money earn it, as you'll find out one day."

"I will?" He caught her arms roughly. "What do you mean?"

"I mean that Nina wants what you have, not what you are," she replied with a sad smile.

"Nina loves me," he said.

"No."

"What does it matter to you, anyway?" he growled. "I haven't been able to turn around without running into you for the past two months. You're always here, getting in the way! What's the matter, did you decide that one kiss wasn't enough, and you're hot for more?"

In fact, it had been the other way around. He'd wanted her so desperately that his mind had gone into hiding, behind the anger he used to disguise the hunger that was driving him mad.

He pulled her into his arms, angry at life and circumstances, ignoring her faint struggles. "God forbid that you should go away with nothing," he added. And he kissed her with all his fury and frustration in his lips. He accused her of chasing him, of wanting his uncle's money. And then he turned around and walked off, leaving her in tears.

His eyes closed as he came back to the present, hating the memory, hating his cruelty. He'd been a different man then, a colder, less feeling man. It had irritated him that Meredith disturbed him physically, that he could be aroused by the sound of her voice, by the sight of her. Because of what he thought he felt for Nina, he'd pushed his growing attraction to Meredith out of his mind. Nina loved him and Meredith just wanted what he had—or so he'd been sure at the time. Now he knew better, and it was too late.

Those few minutes he'd made love to Meredith in the stable that long-ago afternoon had been the sweetest and saddest of his entire life. He'd been cruel after the will was read because he'd felt betrayed by his uncle and by her. But he'd also been sad, because he wanted Meredith far more than Nina. He'd given his word to Nina that he was going to marry her, and honor made him stick to it. So he'd forced Meredith to run away to remove the temptation from his path. He'd known deep inside that he couldn't have resisted Meredith much longer. And he had no right to her.

It struck him as odd that he'd lost control with Meredith. He'd never lost it with Nina, although he'd had a lukewarm kind of feeling for her that had grown out of her adoration and teasing. But what he'd felt with Meredith had been fire and storm. The last time he'd seen her, he'd raged at her that she'd tempted him by following him around like a lovesick puppy, and that had been the last straw. She'd run then, all right, and she hadn't stopped. Not for five years. A week after she left, an attorney brought him the stock, legally signed over to him without a single request for money. Nina had been delighted, and she'd led him right to the altar. He'd been so cut up by his own conscience about what he'd done to Meredith that he hadn't protested, even though his yen for Nina had all but left him.

He went through the motions of making love to Nina, but it wasn't at all satisfying to him. And she always smiled at him so lovingly when they were in bed together. Smiling. Until the day the court battle started, initiated by his cousins, and he was backed into a corner that Nina didn't think he'd get out of. So she left him and divorced him, and he'd had years to regret his own foolishness.

Meredith's attitude toward him in the shop hadn't really come as a surprise. He knew how badly he'd hurt her that day, frightened her. Probably she'd never had a lover or wanted one, because if appearances were anything to go by, he'd left some bad scars. He felt even guiltier about that. But it didn't seem as if he were going to get close enough to tell her the truth about what had happened— even if his pride would allow it.

And anyway, she'd made her feelings about the house clear. She wouldn't voluntarily set foot in it. He sighed heavily. Incredible, he thought, how a man could become his own worst enemy. Looking back, he knew his uncle had been right. If he'd married Meredith, she'd have loved him, and in time he might have been able to love her back. As things stood, that was something he'd never know.

Down the road at Bobby and Bess's house, Meredith Calhoun was halfheartedly watching a movie on Bess's VCR as she tried to come to grips with the unexpected confrontation with Blake.

She felt shaky inside. The sight of Blake, with his jet black hair, green eyes and arrogant, mocking smile, had twisted her heart. Over the years she'd tried to force herself to go out on dates, see other men. But it hadn't worked. She couldn't bear for any man to do more than kiss her, and even the kisses were bitter and unpleasant after Blake's. One part of her was afraid of Blake because of what he'd done to her, but another part remembered the first kiss in the stable, the sweet, slow hunger that had flared between them like summer lightning. And because of that kiss, no other man had ever been able to stir her.

Blake's daughter had come as the biggest surprise. Meredith hadn't known about the child. It seemed, from what Elissa said, that nobody had. Sarah Jane was a quirk of fate, and she wondered if Blake still loved Nina. If he did, Sarah Jane would be a comfort to him. But when he'd said that Nina was dead, it had been without a scrap of emotion in his face or his eyes. He didn't seem to care one way or another. That was strange, because he'd been so adamant about marrying Nina, so certain that she loved him.

Meredith got up, oblivious to the television, and began to wander restlessly around Bess's big living room. She stopped in front of the picture window. Beyond it, on a rise a few hundred yards away, was Blake's house. She sighed, remembering the happy times she'd had there before the will had been read. Blake had always seemed to resent her, but that day in the stable had been full of soft magic. Because of it, she'd actually expected something more from him than anger. She'd dreamed afterward that he'd left Nina and discovered that he loved Meredith and couldn't live without her. Dreams.

She laughed with a new cynicism. That would be the day, when Blake Donavan would feel anything but dislike for her. He hadn't been openly antagonistic today, but he'd verged on it just before she left the store. Sarah liked her and it was going to be difficult to keep the child at bay without hurting her. Meredith had a feeling that Sarah Jane's young life hadn't been a happy one. She didn't act like a contented child, and apparently she'd only been with Blake and Mrs. Jackson for a day or so. Meredith had wondered why, but hadn't dared ask Blake.

Sarah reminded her of herself at that age, a poor little kid from the wrong side of the tracks, with no brothers or sisters and parents who worked themselves into early graves trying to make a living with the sweat of their brows. Bess had been her only friend, and Bess had it even worse than she did at home. The two of them had become

close as children and remained close as adults. So when
Bess had invited Meredith, with Bobby's blessing, to come
and stay for a few weeks, she'd welcomed the rest from
work and routine.

She hadn't consciously considered that Blake was going
to be a very big part of her visit. She'd actually thought she
could come to Jack's Corner without having to see him at
all. Which was silly. King and Elissa and Bess and Bobby
all knew him, and Blake and King were best friends. She
wondered if maybe she'd rationalized things because of
Blake, because she'd wanted to see him again, to see if her
fears had been real or just manifestations of unrequited
love and sorrow. She wanted to see if looking at him could
still make her knees go weak and her heart run away.

Well, now she knew. It could. And if she had any sense
of self-preservation, she was going to have to keep some
distance from him. She couldn't risk letting Blake get close
to her heart a second time. Once had been enough—more
than enough. She'd just avoid him, she told herself, and
everything would be all right.

But avoiding him turned out to be a forlorn hope, because Sarah Jane liked Meredith and contrived to get her
father to call Elissa about that visit she'd mentioned.

Blake listened to the request with mixed feelings. Sarah
Jane was beginning to settle down a little, although she was
still belligerent and not an overly joyful addition to the
household. Mrs. Jackson was coping well enough, but
she'd vanish the minute Blake came home from work,
leaving him to try and talk to his sullen young daughter. He
knew that the situation needed a woman's touch, but Mrs.
Jackson wasn't the woman. Meredith already liked Sarah,
and Sarah was drawn to her. If he could get Meredith to
befriend the child, it would make his life easier. But in another way, he was uncertain about trying to force himself

and Sarah on Meredith. After having seen how frightened she still was of him, how bitter she was about the past, he might open old wounds and rub salt in them. He didn't want to hurt Meredith, but Sarah Jane was driving him nuts, and he needed help.

"You have to call 'lissa," Sarah Jane said firmly, her mutinous mouth pouting up at him. "She promised I could play with her little girl. I want to see Mer'dith, too. She likes me." She glared at him, her eyes so like his only in her youthful face. "You don't like me."

"I explained that to you," he said with exaggerated patience as he perched on the corner of his desk. "We don't know each other."

"You don't ever come home," she said, sighing. "And Mrs. Jackson doesn't like me, either."

"She's not used to children, Sarah, any more than I am." A corner of his mouth twisted. "Look, sprout, I'll try to spend more time with you. But you've got to understand that I'm a busy man. A lot of people depend on me."

"Can't you call 'lissa?" she persisted. "Please?" she added. "Please?"

He found himself picking up the telephone. Sarah had a knack for getting under his skin. He was beginning to get used to the sound of her voice, the running footsteps in the morning, the sound of cartoons and children's programs coming from the living room. Maybe in time he and Sarah would get along better. They were still in the squaring off and glaring stages right now, and she was every bit as stubborn as he was.

He talked to Elissa, who was delighted to comply with Sarah's request. She promised to set things up for the following morning because it was Saturday and Blake could bring Sarah down to Bess's house. But first she wanted to check with Bess and make sure it was all right.

Blake and Sarah both waited for the phone to ring. Blake wondered how Meredith was going to feel about it, but apparently she didn't mind, because Elissa had called back within five minutes and said that Bess would be expecting the child about ten o'clock. Not only that, Sarah was invited to spend the day.

"I can spend the day?" Sarah asked, brightening.

"We'll see." Blake was noncommittal. "Why don't you find something to play with?"

Sarah shrugged. "I don't have any toys. I had a teddy bear, but he got lost and Daddy Brad wouldn't let me look for him before they brought me here."

His eyes narrowed. "Don't call him that again," he said gruffly. "He isn't your father. I am."

Sarah's eyes widened at his tone, and he felt uncomfortable for having said anything at all.

"Can I call you 'Daddy'?" Sarah asked after a long minute.

Blake's breath caught in his throat. He shifted. "I don't care," he said impassively. In fact, he did care. He cared like hell.

"Okay," she said, and went off to the kitchen to see if Mrs. Jackson had any more cookies.

Blake frowned, thinking about what she'd said about toys. Surely a child of almost four still played with them. He'd have to ask Elissa. She'd know about toys and little girls.

The next morning, Sarah dressed herself in her new frilly dress and her shoes and went downstairs. Blake had to bite his lip to keep from howling. She had the dress on backward and unbuttoned. She had on frilly socks, but one was yellow and one was pink. Her hair was unruly, and the picture she made was of chaos, not femininity.

"Come here, sprout, and let's get the dress on properly," he said.

She glared at him. "It's all right."

"No, it's not." He stood. "Don't argue with me, kid. I'm twice your size."

"I don't have to mind you," she said.

"Yes, you do. Or else."

"Or else what?" she challenged.

He stared down at her. "Or else you'll stay home today."

She grimaced and stared down at the carpet. "Okay."

He helped her turn the dress around and cursed under his breath while he did up buttons that were hard for his big, lean hands to work. He finally got them fixed, then took her upstairs, where he searched until he found matching socks and then brushed her straight hair until it looked soft and shiny.

She turned before he finished, looking small and oddly vulnerable on the vanity stool, and her green eyes met his. "I never had any little children to play with. My mommy said I made her nervous."

He didn't say anything, but he could imagine Nina being uncomfortable around children.

"Can I stay here?" Sarah asked unexpectedly, and there was a flash of real fear in her eyes. "You won't make me go away, will you?"

He had to bite down hard to keep back a harsh curse. "No, I won't make you go away," he said after a minute. "You're my daughter."

"You didn't want me when I was a baby," she accused mutinously.

"I didn't know about you," he said, sitting down and talking to her very seriously, as if she were already an adult. "I didn't know I had a little girl. Now I do. You're a Donavan, and this is your place in the world. Here, with me."

"And I can live here forever?"

"Until you grow up, anyway," he promised. His green eyes narrowed. "You aren't going to start crying or anything, are you?" he asked, because her eyes were glistening.

That snapped her out of it. She glared at him. "I never cry. I'm brave."

"I guess you've had to be, haven't you?" he murmured absently. He stood. "Well, if we're going, let's go. And you be on your best behavior. I'm going to tell Bess to swat you if you don't mind her."

"Mer'dith won't let her hit me," she said smugly. "She's my friend. Do you have any friends?"

"One or two," he said, holding her hand as they went down the long staircase.

"Do they come to play with you?" she asked seriously. "And could they play with me, too?"

He chuckled deep in his throat, trying to imagine King Roper sitting cross-legged on the living room carpet, dressing a doll.

"I don't think so," he replied. "They're grown-ups."

"Oh. Grown-ups are too big to play, I guess. I don't want to grow up. I wish I had a doll."

"What kind of doll?" he asked.

"A pretty one with long golden hair and pretty dresses. I could talk to her. And a teddy bear," she said sadly. "I want a teddy bear just like Mr. Friend. I miss Mr. Friend. He used to sleep with me. I'm ascared of the dark," she added.

"Yes, I know," he murmured, having had to help Mrs. Jackson get her to bed every night and chase out the monsters before she closed her eyes.

"Lots of monsters live in my room," she informed him. "You have to kill them every night, don't you?"

"So far, I'm ahead by one monster," he reassured her.

"You're awful big," she said, eyeing him with an unblinking scrutiny. "I bet you weigh one million pounds."

"Not quite."

"I'm ten feet tall," she said, going on tiptoe.

He led her out the door, calling goodbye to Mrs. Jackson. It seemed natural to hold her hand and smile at her chatter. There was magic in a child, even a hard case like this one. He wondered if security would soften her, and doubted it. She had spirit and inner strength. Those qualities pleased him. She'd need them if she lived with him.

Bess and Bobby's house was a split-level brick with exquisite landscaping and a small thicket of trees that separated their property from Blake's. In the driveway were Elissa's gray Lincoln, Meredith's red Porsche convertible and the blue Mercedes that Bess drove. Blake parked behind them on the long driveway and helped Sarah out.

She was at the front door before he reached it, excited as the door opened and a little blond girl about her age shyly greeted her.

"This is Danielle, Sarah. She's looked forward to meeting you," Elissa said with a smile. "Hi, Blake. Come on in."

He took off his gray Stetson and stood in the hall while Sarah went into the living room with Danielle, who'd brought a box of toys with her.

Sarah's eyes lit up like a Christmas tree, and she exclaimed over every single one of Danielle's things, as if she'd never seen toys before. She sat down on the carpet and handled each one gingerly, turning it over and examining it and telling Danielle how beautiful the dolls were.

"She doesn't have any toys," Blake told Elissa with a worried frown. "She seems so mature sometimes. I didn't realize..."

"Parenthood takes time," Elissa assured him. "Don't expect to learn everything at once."

"I don't think I've learned anything yet," he confessed. He frowned as he watched his daughter. "I expected her to push Danielle around and try to take her toys away. She isn't the easiest child to get along with."

"She's a frightened child," Elissa replied. "Underneath there are some sweet qualities. You see, she's playing very nicely, and she isn't causing trouble."

"Yet," Blake murmured, waiting for the explosion to come.

His head turned as Meredith came down the hall. She hesitated momentarily, then joined them.

"Bess is getting coffee," she said quietly. She was wearing a pale green sundress that slashed squarely over her high breasts, and her hair was loose, waving around her shoulders. She looked younger this way, and Blake almost sighed with memories.

"Will you stay and have a cup with us?" Elissa asked him.

"I guess so," he agreed. His eyes hadn't left Meredith.

She averted her gaze and started into the living room, too vulnerable to risk letting him see how easily he could get to her with that level, unblinking stare.

"Mer'dith!" Sarah jumped up, all eyes and laughing smile, and ran with her arms open to be picked up and hugged warmly. "Oh, Mer'dith, Daddy brought me to see Dani and he's going to get me another Mr. Friend and he says I can have a doll! Oh, he's just the nicest daddy...!"

Blake looked as if someone had poured ice into his shirt. He stared at the child blankly. She'd just called him

'Daddy' for the first time, and something stirred in the region of his heart, making him feel warm and needed. It was a new feeling, as if he weren't totally alone anymore.

"That's nice, darling," Meredith was telling the child. She let her down and knelt beside her, smiling as she pushed back Sarah's unruly hair. "You look very pretty this morning. I like your new dress."

"It's very pretty," Danielle agreed. She was dressed in slacks and a shirt for playing, but she didn't make fun of Sarah's dress. She was a quiet child and sweet natured.

"I put it on backward, but Daddy fixed it for me." She smiled at Meredith. "Can you stay and play with us? We can play with dolls."

"I wish I could," Meredith said, nervous because Blake was watching her so closely. She was frantic for a way out of the house, away from him. "But I have to go into town to the library and do some research."

"I thought this was supposed to be a holiday," Bess said as she came in with a tray of coffee and cake. "You're here to rest, not to work."

Meredith smiled at her lovely blond friend. "I know. But I'm not comfortable if I don't have something to do. I won't be long."

"I could drive you," Blake volunteered.

She blanched and started to refuse, but Elissa and Bess jumped in and teased and cajoled until they made it impossible for her to turn down his offer.

She wanted to scream. Alone with Blake in his car? What would they say to each other? What could they say to each other that wouldn't involve them in another terrible argument? The past was very much in Meredith's thoughts, and she wasn't about to risk a repeat of it. But she'd allowed herself to be manipulated by him, and it looked as though she wasn't going to be able to get out of going to town with him. Now, she thought, what are you going to do?

Four

Blake could sense the nervousness in Meredith as she sat stiffly in the seat beside him while he started the car. In the old days, he might have made some cutting remark about it, but the days were gone when he'd deliberately try to hurt her.

"Fasten your seat belt," he said, noticing that she hadn't.

"Oh." She did it absently. "I usually remember in my own car," she said with faint defensiveness.

"Don't you ever ride with other people?"

"Not if I can help it," she murmured, glancing at his hard profile as he backed the car out of the driveway and pulled onto the highway.

"Are your friends bad drivers," he asked, "or is it that you just don't like being out of control?"

"Who drives you, if we're going to throw stones?" she asked with a pleasantly cool smile.

His mouth twitched. "Nobody."

She toyed with her white leather purse, twisting the thin strap around her fingers while she stared out the window at the green crops and grazing cattle on the way to Jack's Corner. The flat horizon seemed to stretch forever, just as it did back in Texas.

"Sarah engineered this get-together," he remarked. "She damned near drove me crazy until I phoned Elissa to arrange it." His green eyes touched her stiff profile and went back to the road. "She likes you."

"I like her, too," she said quietly. "She's a sweet child."

"'Sweet' isn't exactly the word I'd choose."

"Can't you see what's under the belligerence?" she asked solemnly, and turned in the seat slightly so that she could look at him without having to move her head. "She's frightened."

"Elissa said that, too. What is she frightened of? Me?" he asked.

"I don't know what," she said. "I don't know anything about the situation, and I'm not prying." She stared at the clasp on her purse and unsnapped it. "She doesn't look like a happy child. And the way she enthused over Danielle's things, I'd almost bet she's hardly had a toy in her life."

"I'm a bachelor," he muttered angrily. "I don't know about children and toys and dresses. My God, until a few days ago I didn't even know I was a father."

Meredith wanted to ask why Nina had kept Sarah's existence a secret, but she didn't feel comfortable talking about such personal things with him. She had to remember that he was the enemy, in a very real sense. She couldn't afford to show any interest in his life.

He was already figuring that out by himself. She either didn't care about how he'd found out, or she wasn't going to risk asking him. He wished he smoked. She made him nervous and he didn't have anything to do with his hands except grip the steering wheel as he drove.

"Mrs. Jackson is one of your biggest fans," he said, moving the conversation away from Sarah.

"Is she? I'm glad."

"I guess you make a fair living from what you do, if that Porsche is any indication."

She lifted her eyes to his face, letting them run over his craggy features. The broken nose was prominent, as was that angry scar down his cheek. She felt a surge of warmth remembering how he'd come by that scar. Her eyes fell.

"I make a good living," she replied. "I'm rather well-to-do, in fact. So if you think I came home looking for a rich husband, you're well off the mark. You're perfectly safe, Blake," she added coldly. "I'm the last woman on earth you'll have to ward off these days."

He had to clamp down hard on his teeth to keep from saying what came naturally. The past was dead, but she had every reason for digging it up and throwing it at him. He had to remember that. If she'd done to him what he'd done to her, he'd have wanted a much worse revenge than a few pithy remarks.

"I don't flatter myself that you'd come looking for me without a loaded gun, Meredith," he returned. He glanced at her, noting the surprise on her face.

She looked out the window again, puzzled and confused.

He pulled the Mercedes into the parking lot behind the library and shut off the engine.

"Don't do that. Not yet," he said when she started to open the door. "Let's talk for a minute."

"What do we have to say to each other?" she asked distantly. "We're different people now. Let the past take care of itself. I don't want to remember—" she stopped short when she realized what she'd blurted out.

"I know." He leaned back against his door, his pale green eyes under thick black lashes searching her face. "I guess you think I was rough with you in the stable deliberately. And I said some cruel things, didn't I?"

She flushed and averted her eyes, focusing on his chest. "Yes," she said, taut with embarrassment and vivid memories.

"It wasn't planned," he replied. "And what I said wasn't what I felt." He sighed heavily. "I wanted you, Meredith. Wanted you with a passion that drove me right over the edge. But I'm sorry I hurt you."

"Nothing happened," she said icily. In her nervousness her hands gripped her purse like talons.

"Only because my uncle came driving up at the right moment," he said bitterly. He studied her set features. "You'll never know how it's haunted me all these long years. I was deliberately rough with you the day the will was read because guilt was eating me up. I'd promised to marry Nina, my cousins were talking lawsuits...and on top of all that, I'd just discovered that I wanted you to the point of madness."

"I don't want to talk about it," she said under her breath. Her eyes closed in pain. "I can't...talk about it."

His eyes narrowed. "I thought Nina loved me," he said gently. "She said she did, and all her actions seemed to prove it. I thought you only wanted the inheritance, that I was a stepping stone for you, a way to escape the poverty you'd lived in all your young life." He ran his fingers lightly over the steering wheel. "It wasn't until after...that day, that the lawyer told me why my uncle had wanted me to marry you." His eyes slid to catch hers and hold them. "I didn't know you were in love with me."

Her face lost every vestige of color. She sat and stared at him, her pride in rags, her deepest secret naked to his scrutiny.

"It wouldn't have made the slightest bit of difference," she choked out. "Nothing would have changed. Except that you'd have used the information to humiliate me even more. You and Nina would have laughed yourselves sick over that irony."

The cynicism in her tone made him feel even guiltier. She'd grown a shell, just like the one he'd lived inside most of his life. It kept people from getting too close, from wounding too deeply. Nina hadn't managed to penetrate it, but Meredith very nearly had. He'd pushed her out of his life at exactly the right moment, because it wouldn't have taken much to give her a stranglehold on his heart. He'd known that five years ago, and did everything he could to prevent it.

Now he was seeing the consequences of his reticence. His life had altered, and so had Meredith's. Her fame must have been poor recompense for the home and children she'd always wanted, for a husband to love and take care of and be loved by.

He couldn't answer her accusation without giving himself away, so he ignored it and let her think what she liked.

"You never used to be sarcastic," he said quietly. "You were quiet and shy—"

"And dull and plain," she added for him with a cold smile. "I still am all those things. But I write books that sell like hotcakes and I've got my own small following of loyal readers. I'm famous and I'm rich. So now it doesn't matter if I'm not a blond bombshell. I've learned to live with what I am."

"Have you?" He searched her eyes for a long moment. "You've learned to hide yourself away from the world so that you won't get hurt. You draw back from emotion, from involvement. Even today you were thinking of ways to keep Sarah from having any time with you. That's the whole point of this trip to the library. Your damned research could have been anytime, but you preferred not to be around while Sarah and I were at Bess's house.''

''All right, maybe I did!'' she said, goaded into telling the truth. ''Sarah is a sweet child, and I could love her, but I don't want to have to look at you, much less be dragged up to that house when you're there. Mars wouldn't be far enough away from you to suit me!''

He was grateful that he'd learned to keep a poker face. She couldn't have known how those words hurt him. She had every reason to want to avoid him, to hate him. But he didn't want to avoid her, and hatred was the last emotion he felt for her now.

''So Sarah's going to have to pay because you don't want to be around me,'' he replied.

She glared at him. ''Oh, no, you don't,'' she said. ''You aren't laying any guilt trips on me. Sarah has you and Mrs. Jackson—''

''Sarah doesn't like me and Mrs. Jackson,'' he interrupted. ''She likes you. She's done nothing but talk about you.''

She turned away. ''I can't,'' she said huskily.

''She could have been our child,'' he said unexpectedly. ''Yours and mine. And that's what's eating you alive, isn't it?''

She couldn't believe he'd said that. She looked back at him with tears welling in her gray eyes, blinding her. ''Damn you!''

''I saw it in your face this morning when you looked at her,'' he went on relentlessly, driven to make her admit it. ''It isn't fear of me that's stopping you—it's fear of admitting that Sarah reminds you too painfully of what you wanted and couldn't have."

She cried out as if he'd slapped her. She pushed the door open and ran toward the library, almost stumbling in her haste to get away from him. She made it to the lobby and stood there shaking, grateful that the librarian was away from the desk as she tried to get her composure back. She fumbled a handkerchief out of her purse and wiped her eyes. Blake was right. She was avoiding Sarah Jane because of the pain the child caused her. But knowing the truth didn't help. It only made things worse that he should be perceptive enough to sense what she was thinking.

She put the handkerchief away and went back to the reading room to pore over volumes on southwestern history. She didn't know how she was going to get back home. Blake would have gone and she'd just have to call Elissa or Bess.

An hour later, calmer and less flustered, she put the notebook she'd been scribbling in back in her purse, returned the reference books to the shelf and walked outside to find a public telephone.

Blake was there, leaning comfortably against the wall, waiting.

"Are you ready to go?" he asked pleasantly as if nothing at all had happened.

She stared at him. "I thought you'd gone."

His broad shoulders rose and fell. "It's Saturday," he said. "I don't usually work on Saturday unless I have to." His eyes narrowed as he searched her face. "Are you all right?" he added quietly.

She nodded, her eyes avoiding him.

"I won't do that again, Meredith," he said deeply. "I didn't mean to upset you. Let's go."

She sat rigidly beside him on the ride home, afraid that he might start on her again despite what he'd said. But he didn't. He turned on the radio and kept it playing until he pulled into Bess's driveway again.

"You don't have to worry," he said before she got out of the car, and there was a resigned expression on his face. "I won't try to force you into a relationship with Sarah. She's my responsibility, not yours."

And that was that. Meredith went back into the house, and after he'd explained to Elissa and Bess that they could call him when Sarah was ready to come home, he drove off.

He didn't know what he was going to do as he drove away. He hadn't expected Meredith to react like that to his words. What he'd said had only been a shot in the dark, but he'd scored a hit. Sarah disturbed her. The child reminded her of Blake's cruelty, and Meredith was going to keep Sarah at a distance no matter what it took.

That was going to be sad for both of them. Meredith had grown cold and self-contained. She could use a child's magic to bring her back into the sunlight. Sarah likewise would profit from Meredith's tenderness. But it wasn't going to happen and he had to face it. He'd hoped that he might reach Meredith again through Sarah, but she wanted no part of him. She hated him.

He went back to the house and locked himself in his study with his paperwork, forcing his mind not to dwell on Meredith's anger. He had no one to blame but himself. And only time would tell if she could ever forgive him.

Later that afternoon, Meredith sat with Bess and Elissa and watched the little girls play.

"Isn't she the image of Blake?" Elissa smiled as she watched Sarah. "I guess it's hard for him, trying to raise a child on his own."

"He needs to marry again," Bess agreed.

"Well, he's rich enough to attract a wife," Meredith replied with cool disinterest.

"Another Nina would be the end of him," Elissa said. "And think of Sarah. She needs to be loved, not pushed aside. She looks as if she's never really been loved."

"She won't be with Blake," Meredith said. "He isn't a loving man."

Elissa looked at her curiously. "Considering his life so far, is that surprising? He's never been loved, has he? Even his uncle manipulated him, used him for the good of the real estate corporation. Blake has been an outsider looking in. He hasn't known how to love. Maybe Sarah will teach him. She's not the little terror she makes out to be. There's an odd softness about her, especially when she talks to Blake. And have you noticed how unselfish she is?" she added. "She hasn't fought with Dani or tried to take her toys away or break them. She's not what she seems."

"I noticed that, too," Meredith said reluctantly. She looked at the child who was so much like Blake and so little like her beautiful blond mother. Her heart ached at the sight of the little girl who could have been her own. If only Blake could have loved her. She smiled sadly. Oh, if only.

Sarah seemed to feel that scrutiny, because she got up and went to Meredith, her curious eyes searching the woman's. "Can you write a book about a little girl and she can have a daddy and mommy to love her?" she asked. "And it could have a pony in it, and lots of dolls like Dani has."

Meredith touched the small, dark head gently. "I might do that," she said, smiling involuntarily.

Sarah smiled back. "I like you, Merry."

She went back to play with Danielle, leaving a hopelessly touched Meredith staring hungrily at her. Tears stung her eyes.

"Merry, could you watch the girls for a bit while Elissa and I run down to the ice cream shop and get some cones for them?" Bess asked with a quickly concealed conspiratorial wink at Elissa.

"Of course," Meredith agreed.

"We won't be a minute," Bess promised. "Do you want a cone?"

"Yes, please. Chocolate." Meredith grinned.

"I want chocolate, too," Sarah pleaded. "A big one."

"I want vanilla," Danielle said.

"Forty-eight flavors, and we live with purists." Bess sighed, shaking her head. "Okay, chocolate and vanilla it is. Won't be a minute!"

Of course it was more than a minute. They were gone for almost an hour, and when they got back, Meredith was sitting in the middle of the carpet with Sarah and Danielle, helping them dress one of Danielle's dolls. Sarah was sitting as close as she could get to Meredith, and her young face was for once without its customary sulky look. She was laughing, and almost pretty.

The ice cream was passed out and another hour went by before Elissa said reluctantly that she and Danielle would have to go.

"I hate to, but King's bringing one of his business associates home for supper, and I have to get Danielle's bath and have her in bed by the time they get home," Elissa said. "But we'll have to do this again."

"Do you have to go?" Sarah asked Danielle sadly. "I wish you could come live with me, and we could be sisters."

"Me, too," Danielle said.

"I like your toys. I guess your mommy and daddy like you a lot."

"Your daddy likes you, too, Sarah," Meredith said gently, taking the child's hand in hers. "He just didn't know that you wanted toys. He'll buy you some of your own."

"Will he, truly?" Sarah asked her, all eyes.

"Truly," she replied, hoping she was right. The Blake she'd known in the past wouldn't have cared overmuch about a child's needs. Of course, the man she'd glimpsed today might. She could hardly reconcile what she knew about him with what she was learning about him.

"That's right," Bess agreed, smiling down at Sarah. "Your dad's a pretty nice guy. We all like him, don't we, Meredith?"

Meredith glared at her. "Oh, we surely do," she said through her teeth. "He's a prince."

Which was what Sarah Jane told her daddy that very night over the supper table. He'd picked her up at Bess's house, but Meredith's car was gone. She was avoiding him, he supposed wearily, and he listened halfheartedly to Sarah all the way home. Now she was telling him about the wonderful time she'd had playing dolls with Meredith, and he turned his attention from business problems to stare at her blankly as what she was saying began to register.

"She did *what*?" he asked.

"She played dolls with me," she said, "and she says you're a prince. Does that mean you used to be a frog, Daddy?" Sarah added. "Because the princess kisses the frog and he turns into a prince. Did my mommy kiss you?''

"Occasionally, and no, I wasn't a frog. Meredith played dolls with you?'' he asked, feeling a tiny glow deep inside himself.

"She really did.'' Sarah sighed. "I like Mer'dith. I wish she was my mommy. Can't she come to live with us?''

He couldn't explain that very easily. "No,'' he said simply. "You'd better get ready for bed.''

"But, Daddy...'' she moaned.

"Go on. No arguments.''

"All right,'' she grumbled. But she went.

He looked after her, smiling faintly. She was a handful, but she was slowly growing on him.

He stayed home on Sunday and took Sarah Jane out to see the horses grazing in the pasture. One of the men, a grizzled old wrangler named Manolo, was working a gelding in the corral, breaking him slowly and gently to the saddle. Blake had complained that Manolo took too long to break horses, especially when he was doing it for the remuda in spring before roundup. The cowhands had to have a string of horses when they started working cattle. But Manolo used his own methods, despite the boss's arguments. No way, he informed Blake, was he going to mistreat a horse just to break it to saddle, and if Blake didn't like that, he could fire him.

Blake hadn't said another word about it. The horses Manolo broke were always gentle and easily managed.

But this horse was giving the old man a lot of trouble. It pranced and reared, and Blake was watching it instead of Sarah Jane when the lacy handkerchief Meredith had given her blew into the corral.

Like a shot, she climbed through the fence to go after it, just as the horse broke away from Manalo and came snorting and bucking in her direction.

Blake saw her and blinked, not believing what his eyes were telling him. All at once he was over the fence, just as Manolo yelled.

Sarah was holding her handkerchief, staring dumbly at the approaching horse.

Blake grabbed her and sent her through the fence, following her with an economy of motion. He thanked God for his own strength as it prevented what would have been a total disaster.

Sarah Jane clung to his neck tightly, crying with great sobs.

He hugged her to him, his eyes closed, a shudder running through his lean, fit body. Another few seconds and it would have been all over. Sarah would have become a tragic memory. It didn't bear thinking about. Worse than that, it brought back an older memory, of another incident with a bronc. He touched his lean cheek where the scar cut across his tan. How many years ago had it been that he'd saved Meredith just as he'd saved Sarah? A long time ago—long before the sight of her began to make him ache.

The fear he'd experienced, added to the unwanted memories, made him furious. He let go of Sarah and held her in front of him, his green eyes glittering with rage.

"Don't you know better than to go into the corral with a wild animal?" he snapped. "Where's your mind, Sarah?"

She stared at him as if he'd slapped her. Her lower lip trembled. "I had to get my...my hankie, Daddy." She held it up. "See? My pretty hankie that Mer'dith gave me...."

He shook her. "The next time you go near any enclo-
sure with horses or cattle in it, you stay out! Do you understand me?" he asked in a tone that made her small body
jerk with a sob. "You could have been killed!"

"I'm so—sorry," she faltered.

"You should be!" he jerked out. "Now get in the
house."

She started crying, frightened by the way he looked.
"You hate me," she whimpered. "I know you do. You
yelled at me. You're mean and ugly...and...I don't like
you!"

"I don't like you, either, at the moment," he bit off,
glaring down at her, his legs still shaking from the exer-
tion and fear. "Now get going."

"You mean old daddy!" she cried. She turned and ran
wildly for the house as Blake stared after her in a blind
rage.

"Is she all right, boss?" Manolo asked from the fence.
"My God, that was quick! I didn't even see her!"

"Neither did I," Blake confessed. "Not until it was
damned near too late." He let out a rough sigh. "I didn't
mean to be so hard on her, but she's got to learn that
horses and cattle are dangerous. I wanted to make sure she
remembered this."

"She'll remember," Manolo said ruefully, and turned
away before the boss could see the look on his face. Poor
little kid. She needed hugging, not yelling.

Blake went in the house a few minutes later and looked
for Sarah, but she was nowhere in sight. Mrs. Jackson had
heard her come in, but she hadn't seen her because she was
working in the front of the house.

He checked Sarah's bedroom, but she wasn't there,
either. Then he remembered what she'd said about being
locked in the closet when she was bad....

He jerked open the closet door and there she sat, her face red and tear stained, sobbing and looking as if she hadn't a friend in the world.

"Go away," she sniffed.

He got down awkwardly on one knee. "You'll suffocate in here."

"I hate you."

"I don't want anything to happen to you," he said. "The horse could have hurt you very badly."

She touched the dusty lace handkerchief to her red eyes. "You yelled at me."

He grimaced. "You scared me," he muttered, averting his gaze. "I never thought I'd get to you in time."

She sniffed and got up on her knees under the hanging dresses and blouses and slacks. "You didn't want me to get hurt?"

"Of course I didn't want you to get hurt," he snapped, green eyes flashing.

"You're yelling at me again," she said, pouting.

He sighed angrily. "Well, I've been doing it for a lot of years, and I won't change. You'll just have to get used to my temper." He stared at her half-angrily. "I thought I was getting the hang of it, and you had to go crawl in with a bucking bronco and set me back."

"Everybody used to yell at me," she told him solemnly. "But they didn't do it just if I got hurt. They didn't like me."

"I like you. That's why I yelled," he muttered.

She smiled through her tears. "Really and truly?"

He grimaced. "Really and truly." He got up. "Come out of there."

"Are you going to spank me?" she asked.

"No."

"I won't do it again."

"You'd better not." He took her hand and led her downstairs. When Mrs. Jackson found out what had happened, she took a fresh coconut cake out of the pantry, sliced it up and poured Sarah a soft drink. She even smiled. Sarah dried her eyes and smiled back.

On Monday Blake took two hours off at lunch and went to a toy store. He bought an armful of dolls and assorted girlish toys and took them to the house without fully understanding his motives. Maybe it was relief that Sarah was all right or guilt because he'd hurt her.

But she sat down in the living room with her new friends—which included a huge stuffed teddy bear—and the way she handled her toys was enough to bring a tear to the eye. She hugged the teddy bear, then she hugged Blake, who was half delighted and half embarrassed by her exuberance.

"You're just the nicest daddy in the whole world," Sarah Jane said, and she was crying again. She wiped her eyes with her hands. "I have a new Mr. Friend now, and he can help you fight monsters."

"I'll keep that in mind. Behave yourself." He went out the door quickly, more moved than he wanted to admit by his daughter's reception to the impromptu toy surprise.

On the way back to work, he remembered what Sarah had said about Meredith playing dolls with her. Meredith had been trying to keep Sarah at arms' length, so he wondered at her actions. Had he been wrong about Meredith's motives? Had he misjudged what he thought was her reason for avoiding Sarah?

He remembered all too well the feel of Meredith's soft, innocent mouth under his that day in the stable, the wonder in her eyes when he'd lifted his head just briefly to look down at her. And then he'd lost control and frightened her, turning the wonder to panic.

That she'd loved him didn't bear thinking about. At least he and Sarah were closer than ever. But she needed more than a father. Sarah needed a mother. Someone to read her stories, to play with her. Someone like Meredith. It made him feel warm to think of Meredith doing those things with his daughter. In time she might even get over the past and start looking ahead. She might fall in love with him all over again.

His body reacted feverishly to that thought, and as quickly his mind rejected it. He didn't want her to love him. He felt guilt for the way he'd treated her and he still wanted her, but *love* wasn't a word in his vocabulary anymore. It hurt too much.

Letting her get close would be risky. Meredith had every reason in the world to want to get even with him. He scowled. Would Meredith want revenge if he could bring himself to tell her the truth about why he'd been so rough with her?

Not that *he* needed her, he assured himself. It was only that Sarah liked her and needed her. But Meredith wouldn't come to the house. She wasn't going to let him, or Sarah, get close to her, and that was the big hurdle. How, he wondered, could he overcome it?

He worried the thought for two days and still hadn't figured out a solution, when he had to fly to Dallas on business for the day. But fate was on his side.

While he was gone, Mrs. Jackson's only living sister had a heart attack and a neighbor called asking Amie to come to Wichita, Kansas, and help look after her. That left Mrs. Jackson with nobody to look after Sarah. She couldn't take the child with her while she tried to care for a heart patient. She called Elissa, but she and her husband and child were out of town. Bess wouldn't be able to cope with the angry little girl. That left only one person in Jack's Corner who might be willing to try.

Without hesitation, Mrs. Jackson picked up the phone and called Meredith Calhoun.

Five

Sarah Jane was almost dancing with pleasure when Meredith came in the door. She ran to her, arms outstretched, and Meredith instinctively picked her up and hugged her warmly. Maternal instincts she hadn't indulged since Blake had sent her running came to the fore, making her soft.

"Now don't you give Meredith any trouble, young lady," Mrs. Jackson cautioned Sarah Jane. "Meredith, this is my sister's phone number, but I'll call as soon as I know something and tell Mr. Blake what's going on. I hope he won't mind."

"You know very well he won't," Meredith said. "I'm sorry about your sister, but I'm sure she'll be all right."

"Well, we can hope, anyway," Mrs. Jackson said, forcing a smile. "There's my cab. I'll be back as soon as I can."

"Bye, Mrs. Jackson," Sarah called.

She turned at the door and smiled at the little girl. "Goodbye, Sarah. I'll miss you. Thanks again, Merry."

"No problem," Meredith said as the housekeeper left.

"We can play dolls now, Merry," Sarah said enthusiastically, repeating the nickname she'd heard for Meredith as she struggled to be put down. She then led Meredith by the hand into the living room. "Look what my daddy bought me!"

Meredith was pleasantly surprised by the array of dolls. There must have been two dozen of them, surrounding a huge, whimsical tan teddy bear who was wearing one of Blake's Stetsons on his shaggy head.

"He's supposed to be my daddy," Meredith said, pointing to the bear, "since my daddy's away. But actually he's Mr. Friend. My old Mr. Friend got lost, so Daddy bought me a new one."

Meredith sat down on the sofa, smiling as Sarah introduced every one of her new toys to her older friend.

"I dropped the pretty hankie you gave me inside the fence," Sarah explained excitedly, "and a big horse almost ran over me, but my daddy saved me. He yelled at me and I cried and hid in the closet, and he came to find me. He said I mustn't *ever* do it again because he liked me." She laughed. "And then he went to the store and brought me ever so many toys."

Meredith was feeling cold chills at the innocent story. She could imagine how Blake had felt, the fear that had gripped him. She remembered so well the day he'd had to rescue her from a wild horse. She wondered if it had brought back memories for him, too.

Sarah looked up at Meredith. "My daddy has an *awful* temper, Merry."

Meredith knew that already. She remembered his temper very well. A lot of things could spark it, but embarrassment, fear, or any kind of threat were sure to ignite it. She could imagine how frightened Sarah had been of him, but apparently toys could buy forgiveness. She chided herself for that thought. Blake could be unexpectedly kind. It was just that he seemed so cold and self-contained. She wondered if Nina had ever really touched him during their brief marriage, and decided that it was unlikely.

Meredith got down on the floor with Sarah, grateful, as they sprawled on the carpet, that she'd worn jeans and a yellow blouse instead of a dress. She and Sarah dressed dolls and talked for a long time before Meredith got the small girl ready for bed, tucked her in and helped her say her prayers.

"Why do I have to say prayers?" Sarah asked.

"To thank God for all the nice things He does for us." Meredith smiled.

"Daddy talks to God all the time," Sarah said. "Especially when I turn things over or get hurt—"

Meredith fought to keep her expression steady. "That's not what I meant, darling. Now you settle down and we'll talk."

"Okay, Merry." She moved her dark head on the pillow. "Merry, do you like me?"

Meredith looked down at the child she might have had. She smiled sadly, touching Sarah's dark hair gently. "Yes, I like you very much, Sarah Jane Donavan," she replied, smiling.

"I like you, too."

Meredith bent and kissed the clean, shiny face. "Would you like me to read you a story? Have you any books?"

The small face fell. "No. Daddy forgot."

"That's all right, then. I can think of one or two." She sat down on Sarah's bed and proceeded to go through several, doing all the parts in different pitches of her voice, while Sarah giggled.

She was just in the middle of "The Three Bears," doing Baby Bear's voice when Sarah sat up, smiling from ear to ear and cried, "Daddy!"

Meredith felt her face burn, her heart start to pound, as he came into the room, dressed in a gray business suit, sparing her a curious glance as he handed something to Sarah.

"Something from Dallas," he told the child. "It's a puppet."

"I love him, Daddy!"

It was a duck puppet, yellow and white, and Sarah wiggled it on her hand while Blake turned to Meredith with a cool smile.

"Where's Amie?" he asked.

She told him, adding that Amie had promised to phone as soon as she knew something. "She couldn't get Elissa, and there wasn't anyone else, so she asked me."

"We had lots of fun, Daddy!" Sarah told him. "Merry and me played dolls and watched TV together!"

"Thank you for taking the time," Blake said, his whole attitude antagonistic. He'd done nothing but think about the irritating woman for days. And there she sat, looking as cool as a cucumber without a hint of warmth in her cold gray eyes, while his body had gone taut and started throbbing at the very sight of her.

Meredith got to her feet, avoiding him. "I didn't mind. Good night, Sarah," she said, running a nervous hand through her loosened dark hair to get it out of her face.

"Good night, Merry. Will you come back to see me again?"

"When I can, darling," she replied absently, without noticing the reaction that endearment had on Blake. "Sleep tight."

"Go to sleep now, young lady," Blake told his daughter.

"But, Daddy, what about the monsters?" Sarah wailed when he started to turn out the light at the door.

He stopped and looked uncomfortable. He wasn't about to start chasing monsters from under the bed and dragging them out of the closet in front of Meredith. Sarah loved the pretend housecleaning and he'd grown used to doing it to amuse her, but a man had to have his secrets. He cleared his throat. "When I walk Meredith to her car, okay?"

That pacified Sarah. She smiled. "Okay, Daddy." She looked at Meredith. "He kills the monsters every night so they won't hurt me. He's very brave and he weighs one million pounds!"

Meredith glanced at Blake and her face went red as she tried to smother laughter. He glared at her, breaking the spell. She rushed out into the hall and kept going.

He caught up with her downstairs and walked her out onto the porch.

"I'm sorry Amie involved you," he said curtly. "Bess would have kept Sarah."

"Bess and Bobby were going out," she replied. "I didn't mind."

"You didn't want to come here, though, even while I was away," he said perceptively. "You don't care for this house very much, do you?"

"Not anymore," she said. "It brings back some painful memories." She moved away from him, but he followed.

"Where's your car?" he asked, searching for it.

"I walked. It was a beautiful night and it's only a short walk."

He glared down at her from his superior height. In his gray suit and pearl-colored Stetson, he looked enormously tall and imposing. He never seemed to smile, she thought, searching his hard features in the light that shone from the windows onto the big, long porch.

"If you're looking for beauty, you won't find it," he said, his mouth twisting into a mocking smile. "The scar only makes it worse."

She gazed at it, the long white line that marred his lean cheek all the way from his high cheekbone to his jaw. "I remember when you got it," she said quietly. "And how."

His expression became grim. "I don't want to talk about it."

"I know." She sighed gently, her eyes searching over his dark face with more poignancy than she knew. "But you were always handsome to me, scar and all," she mused, turning away as the memories came flooding back. "Good night...Blake!"

He'd whipped her around, his lean hands biting into her arms. She was wearing a sleeveless lemon yellow blouse with her jeans, and it made her skin look darker than it was. Where his fingers held her, the flesh went white from the pressure.

"I..." He eased his hold a little, although he didn't release her. "I didn't mean to do that." He drew in a silent breath. "I don't suppose you'll ever get over the fear I caused you in the past, will you?" he added, watching her eyes widen, her body stiffen.

"It was my first intimacy," she whispered, flushing. "And you made it...you were very rough."

"I remember," he replied. His pride fought him when he tried to tell her the truth, although he wanted to. He wanted to make her understand his roughness.

"As you said, it was a long time ago," she added, pulling against his hold gently.

"Not that long. Five years." He searched her eyes. "Meredith, surely you've dated men. There must have been one or two who could stir you."

"I couldn't trust them," she said bitterly. "I was afraid to take a chance with anyone else."

"Most men aren't as rough as I am," he replied coldly.

Her breath was sighing out like a whisper. He made her nervous, and the feel of his hands was affecting her breathing. "Most men aren't as much a man as you are," she breathed, closing her eyes as forgotten sensations worked down her spine and made her ache.

His pride burned with what she'd said. Did she think him masculine, handsome? Or was that all in the past, part of the love he'd killed?

He drew her closer and held her against him warmly but chastely, her legs apart from his. He didn't want her to feel how aroused he already was.

"I'm not much gentler now than I used to be, Meredith," he said deeply, as his head bent toward her. "But I'll try not to frighten you this time...."

She opened her mouth to protest, but his lips met hers. They probed her soft mouth while his lean, strong hands slid up to frame her face.

She stiffened, but only for a minute. The taste of him made her dizzy with pleasure. She liked what he was doing to her too much to protest. After a minute she relaxed, letting his mouth do what it wanted to hers.

"God, it's sweet," he whispered roughly, biting at her lips with more instinct than expertise. His voice was shaking and he didn't care if she heard it. "Oh, God, it's so sweet!"

His mouth ground into hers and his arms slid completely around her. He pulled her body up against his so that his legs touched hers, and he felt her sudden shocked tautness.

He let her move away, his eyes glittering, his breath rustling out of his throat. "I shouldn't have done that," he said gruffly. "I didn't mean to let you feel how aroused I was."

Having him mention it shocked her more than the feel of his body, but she tried not to let him see her reaction. She stepped back, touching her mouth with light fingers. Yes, it had been sweet, as she'd heard him whisper feverishly. Just as it had been five years ago in the stable, when he'd put his mouth on hers and she'd ached to have him touch her.

"I have to get back to Bess's house," she said unsteadily.

"Just a minute." He took her hand and pulled her farther into the light. He held her gaze so that he could see the fear mingled with desire that lingered in her eyes, the swollen softness of her mouth.

"What are you looking for?" she asked huskily.

"You're still afraid of me," he said, his jaw going taut.

"I'm sorry." She lowered her eyes to his chest, to its quick, hard rise and fall. "I can't help it."

"Neither can I," he replied bitterly. He let her go, turning away. "I'm not much good at lovemaking, if you want the truth," he said through his teeth.

That was true. He had the patience, but not the knowledge. Nina had taught him a few things, but she'd been indifferent to his touch and her response to him had always been just lukewarm. She hadn't known he was innocent, but she had known he was inexperienced, and at the end of their relationship she'd taunted him with his lack of expertise. It was one of the things he hated remembering. Better to let Meredith think he was brutal than to have her know how green he was.

Watching him, Meredith was surprised by the admission. She'd always considered him experienced. If he wasn't, it would explain so much.

Suddenly, she understood his fierce pride a little better. She went closer to him, reaching out to lightly touch his sleeve. He jerked a little, as if that impersonal contact went through him like fire.

"It's all right, Blake," she said hesitantly.

He looked down at the slender hand that rested lightly on his sleeve. "I'm like a bull in a china shop," he said unexpectedly, looking into her eyes. "With women."

She felt a surge of emotion at that rough admission. He'd never been more approachable than he was right now. Part of her was wary of him, but another part wanted once, just once, to give in without a fight.

She went up on her tiptoes and pulled his head down to hers. He stiffened and she stopped dead.

"No!" he whispered huskily when she started to draw back in embarrassment. "Go ahead. Do what you want to."

She couldn't believe that he really wanted her to kiss him, but he was giving every indication that he did. She didn't know a lot about it, either, since all she'd ever done with men was kissing.

She drew her lips lightly over Blake's hard ones, teasing them gently. Her breath shook at his mouth while she held his head within reach, but she didn't relent. Her fingers slid into the thick, cool hair at the nape of his strong neck and

her nails slid against his skin while her mouth toyed softly
with his.

"I can't take much of that," he whispered roughly. His
hands held her hips now, an intimacy that she should have
protested, but she was too weak. "Do it properly."

"Not yet," she whispered. Her teeth closed softly on his
lower lip, tugging at it sensuously. She felt him tremble as
her tongue traced his upper lip.

"Meredith," he bit off, and his hands hurt her for an
instant.

"All right." She knew what he wanted, what he needed.
She opened her mouth on his and slid her tongue inside it,
and the reaction she got from him was electrifying.

He cried out. His arms swallowed her, bruising her
against his hard chest. He was trembling. Meredith felt the
soft tremors with exquisite awareness, with pride that she
could arouse him that easily after a beauty like Nina.

"Blake," she whispered under his mouth, and closed her
eyes as she gave him the weight of her body, the warmth of
her mouth.

She felt him move. Her back was suddenly against the
wall and he was easing down over her body.

Her eyes flew open and his head lifted fractionally, and
all the while his body overwhelmed hers, his hips lying
heavy and hard against hers, pressing against her.

She could feel the full strength of his arousal now, and
it should have frightened her, but it didn't. He was slow
and gentle, not impatient at all as his hands slid to her hips,
holding her.

"This should really frighten the hell out of you,
shouldn't it?" he asked huskily, searching her eyes. "You
can feel what I want, and I'm not quite in control right
now."

"You aren't hurting me," she whispered. "And I started it this time."

"So you did." He moved down, letting his mouth repeat the soft, arousing movements hers had made earlier. "Like that, Meredith?" he whispered at her lips. "Is that how you like it?"

"Yes," she whispered back, excitement making her voice husky. Her hands were against his shirt and she could feel the heat from his body under the fabric.

"I want to open my shirt and let you touch me," he whispered roughly. "But that might be the straw that breaks the camel's back, and there's a long, comfortable sofa just a few feet inside the door."

The thought was more than tempting. She could already feel his skin against hers, his body overwhelming hers. She wanted him, and there wasn't really any reason to say no. Except that her pride couldn't take the knowledge that he wanted only her body and nothing else about her.

"I can't sleep with you," she said miserably. She let her head rest against him, drowning in the feel of his body over hers. "Blake, you have to stop," she groaned. "I'm going crazy...!"

"So am I." He pushed himself away from her, breathing roughly. His darkened green eyes looked down into hers. "You wanted me," he said, as if he were only just realizing it.

She flushed and looked up at his hard face. "I don't understand what you want from me."

"Sarah needs a woman's companionship," he said tersely.

"That isn't why you made love to me," she returned, searching his eyes.

He sighed deeply. "No, it isn't." He walked to the edge of the porch and leaned against one of the white columns, looking out over the wide expanse of flat land. The only trees were right around the house, where they'd been planted. Beyond was open land, dotted with a few willows at the creek and a few straggly bushes, but mostly flat and barren all the way to the horizon.

"Why, Blake?" she asked. She had to know what he was after.

"Do you know what an obsession is, Meredith?" he asked a minute later.

"Yes, I think so."

"Well, that's what I feel for you." He shifted so that he could see her. "Obsessed," he repeated, letting his green eyes slide over her sensually. "I don't know why. You aren't beautiful. You aren't even voluptuous. But you arouse me as no other woman ever has or ever will. I couldn't even feel for Nina what I feel for you." He laughed coldly. "After she left me, there wasn't anyone else. I couldn't. I don't want anyone but you."

She didn't know if she was still breathing. The admission knocked the wind out of her, took the strength from her legs. She looked at him helplessly.

"You haven't...seen me in five years," she said, trying to rationalize.

"I've seen you every night," he ground out. "Every time I closed my eyes. My God, don't you remember what I did to you that day in the stable? I stripped you...." He closed his eyes, oblivious to her scarlet face and trembling body. "I looked at you and touched you and put my mouth on you." He bit back a curse and opened his eyes again, tormented. "I see you in my bed every damned night of my life," he breathed. "I want you to the point of madness."

She caught the railing and held on tight. She couldn't believe what she was hearing. It wasn't possible for a man to feel that kind of desire, she told herself. Not when he didn't feel anything emotional for the woman. But Blake was different. As Elissa said, he'd never been loved, so he didn't know what it was. But all men felt desire. A man didn't have to love to want.

"Don't worry—" he laughed mockingly "—I'm not going to force you into anything. I just wanted you to know how I felt. If that sensuous little kiss was some sort of game, you'd better know how dangerous it is. I'm not sane when I touch you. I wouldn't hurt you deliberately for the world, but I want you like hell."

Her swollen lips parted. "I wasn't playing," she said with quiet pride. "It was no game. You..." She hesitated. "You seemed so disturbed because you'd been rough. I wanted to show you that you hadn't made me afraid."

He watched her unblinkingly. "You weren't, were you?" he said then, scowling. "Not even when I brought you close and let you feel what you were doing to me."

She shifted. "You shouldn't have," she murmured evasively.

"Why hide it?" he asked. He moved toward her, encouraged by her response and her lack of bitterness. He was taking a hell of a chance by being honest with her, but it might be his only way of reaching her. "You might as well know it all."

She lifted her face as he stood over her. "Know what?"

"Nina was my first woman," he said bluntly. "And the only woman."

She wanted to sit down, but there was no chair. She leaned against the banister, her eyes searching his hard face. He wasn't kidding. He meant it.

"That's right," he said, nodding when he saw the memories replaying in her eyes. "The day we were in the stable together, I was as inexperienced as you were. That's why I was rough. It wasn't deliberate. I didn't know how to make love."

Her lips opened on a slow breath. "No wonder..." she whispered.

"Yes, no wonder." He brushed a strand of loosened hair from her pale cheek. "Why don't you laugh? Nina did."

She could feel the hurt under that mocking statement. What it must have done to his pride! "Nina was a—" She bit back the word.

He laughed coldly. "She certainly was," he agreed. "She taunted me with it toward the end," he added, his eyes bitter and cynical. "I didn't want to risk that kind of ridicule again, so there weren't any more women."

"Oh, Blake," she whispered, closing her eyes on a wave of pain. "Blake, I'm so sorry!"

"I don't want pity. I wanted you to know the truth. If you're ever tempted to give in to me, you're entitled to know what you'd be up against. My God," he said heavily, moving away, "I don't even know the basics. Books and movies don't make up for experience. And Nina wasn't interested in tutoring me."

"I wish I'd known," she said huskily. "I wish I'd known five years ago."

He looked back at her, his thick eyebrows raised. "Why?"

"I wouldn't have fought you," she said simply. "I thought you were terribly experienced." She lowered her eyes. "I'm sorry. I guess I hurt your ego as much as you frightened me."

He studied her in a tense silence. "You don't have a thing to apologize for. I'm the one who's sorry." He waited until she lifted her head, and he caught her eyes and held them. "You haven't wanted anyone, in all this time?"

"I wanted you," she said frankly. "I...couldn't feel that for anyone else. I'd rather have been frightened by you than pleasured by the greatest lover living." She laughed coldly. "So I guess I'm in the same boat that you are." She clutched her purse. "I really do have to go," she said after a long, quiet moment during which he stared at her without saying anything at all.

He escorted her down the porch steps. "All right. I'll walk you to the woods and watch you through them. Sarah Jane will be all right until I get back, and the house is in full view the whole way."

"Sarah is very much like you," she said.

"Too much like me," he replied. His fingers brushed hers as they walked, accidentally or deliberately she didn't know, making her all too aware of him. "She almost got trampled the other day, climbing into the corral to retrieve a handkerchief."

"She told me. I suppose you were livid."

"Mild word," he said. "I blew up. Scared her. I found her hiding in the closet, and I felt like a dog. I went to town the next day and bought her half a toy store to make up for yelling at her." He sighed. "She scared me blind. I kept thinking what could have happened if my reflexes had been just a bit slower."

"But they weren't." She smiled. "You were always quick in an emergency."

He looked down at her and his fingers lazily entangled themselves in hers. "Luckily for you," he murmured darkly, watching her flush. "I haven't had an easy life," he said then. "I had to be tough to survive. They weren't good days before I came here to live with my uncle. I got in a lot of fights because of my illegitimacy."

"I never heard you talk about that," she said.

"I never could." His fingers tightened in hers as they got to the small wooded area and stopped. "I can't talk about a lot of things, Meredith. Maybe that's why I'm so damned alone."

She glanced toward Bess's house. Bess and Bobby must have come home, because their car was in the driveway next to hers. She hesitated, not eager to leave Blake in this oddly talkative mood. "You've got Sarah now," she reminded him gently.

"Sarah is getting to me," he confessed ruefully. "God, I don't know what I'd do if I could sit down in a chair without crushing a stuffed toy, or go to bed without running monsters out of closets." He smiled mockingly. "It cut me to pieces when she started crying after I raged at her about getting in with the horse."

"She doesn't seem that sensitive at first glance, but she is," she replied. "I noticed it that first day, at the children's shop, and again when she played with Danielle. I gather she was neglected a lot before they sent her to you."

"I got the same feeling. She had a nightmare just after she came here," he recalled quietly. "She woke up in the early hours, screaming her head off, and when I asked what was the matter, she said they wouldn't let her out of the closet." His face hardened, and for an instant he looked relentless. "I've still got half a mind to send my lawyers after that housekeeper."

"A woman that cruel will make her own hell," Meredith said. "Mean people don't get away with anything, Blake. It may seem that they do, but in the end their meanness ricochets back at them."

"The way mine did at me?" he asked with a mirthless laugh. "I scarred you and pushed you out of my life, married Nina, and settled down to what I thought would be wedded bliss. And look where it got me."

"You've got everything," she corrected. "Money, power, position, a sweet little girl."

"I've got nothing except Sarah," he said shortly. His green eyes glittered in the faint light. "I thought I needed money and power to make people accept me. But I'm no more socially acceptable now than I was when I was poor and illegitimate. I've just got more money."

"Acceptance doesn't have anything to do with money." She stared down at the big, warm hand clasping hers. "You're not the world's most sociable man. You keep to yourself and you don't smile very much. You intimidate people." She smiled gently, her eyes almost loving despite her reluctance to give herself away. "That's why you don't get a lot of social invitations. This isn't the Dark Ages. People don't hold the circumstances of their birth against each other anymore. It's a much more open society than it was."

"It stinks," he returned coldly. "Women propositioning men, kids neglected and abused and cast off...."

"They don't burn witches anymore, though," she whispered conspiratorially, going up on tiptoe. "And the stocks have been eliminated, too."

His face cracked into a reluctant smile. "Okay. You've got a point."

"Who propositioned you?" she added.

He cocked his head a little to study her. "A woman at the workshop in Dallas I just came back from. I didn't believe she meant it until she put her room key in an ashtray beside my coffee cup."

"What did you do?" she asked, because she had to know.

He smiled faintly. "Took it out and handed it back." He touched her cheek gently, running a lean finger down it. "I told you on the porch. I don't want anyone but you."

She lowered her eyes to his chest. "I can't, Blake."

"I'm not asking you to." He let go of the hand he was holding. "I'm archaic in my notions, in case it's escaped your notice. I don't seduce virgins."

Her body tingled at the thought of making love with Blake. It was exciting and surprising to know how much he wanted her. But her own conscience wasn't going to let her give in, and he knew that, too.

"I guess you'd rather I got my autographing over and left town..." she began.

He tilted her chin up so he could see her face. "Sarah and I are going on a picnic Saturday. You can come."

The suddenness of the invitation made her blink. "Saturday?"

"We'll pick you up at nine. You can wear jeans. I'm going to."

Her eyes lifted to his. "Blake..."

"I like having things out in the open, so there aren't any more misunderstandings," he said simply. "I want you. You want me. But that's as far as it goes, and there won't be any more of what happened on my porch tonight. I'll keep my hands off and we'll give Sarah a good time. Sarah likes you," he added quietly. "I think you like her, too. She could use a few good memories before you go back to the life you left in San Antonio."

So he was going to freeze her out. He wanted her, but he wasn't going to do anything about it. He wanted her for Sarah, not for himself, despite his hunger for her.

She hesitated. "Is it wise letting her get used to me?" she asked, her voice echoing the disappointment she felt.

His hand on her chin became faintly caressing. "Why not?" he asked.

"It will be another upset for her when I leave," she said.

His thumb moved over her lips, brushing them, caressing them. "How long are you going to stay?"

"Until the first of the month," she said. "I do the autographing a week from Saturday."

His hand fell just in time to keep her from throwing herself against him and begging him to kiss her. "Then you can spend some time with Sarah and me until you leave. I won't force you into any corners and we can help Sarah find her feet."

Her eyes searched his night-shadowed face. "Why do you want me around?"

"God knows," he muttered. "But I do."

She sighed audibly, fighting her need to be near him.

"Don't brood," he said. He didn't smile, but there was something new about the way he was looking at her. "Just take things one day at a time and stop analyzing everything I say."

"Was I doing that? Okay, I'll try." She wished there were more light. She managed a smile. "Good night, Blake."

"Go on. I'll watch you."

She left him standing there and went running down to the house, her heart blazing with new hope.

If there was any chance for her to have Blake, she'd take it willingly, no matter what the risk. She now understood the reasons for his actions. And if she went slowly and didn't ask for the impossible, he might even come to love her one day. She went to sleep on that thought, and her dreams were so vivid that she woke up blushing.

Six

Meredith was awake, dressed and ready to go by eight on Saturday morning, with an hour to kill before it was time for Blake and Sarah to pick her up.

Bess, an early riser herself these days, made breakfast and smiled wickedly at her friend.

"It must feel strange to have Blake ask you out after all these years."

"It does. But I'm not kidding myself that it's out of any great love for me," she said, neglecting to tell Bess that Blake's main interest in her was sensual. All the same, just remembering the way he'd kissed her Wednesday night made her tingle from head to toe. And he'd shared secrets with her that she knew he'd never tell anyone else. That alone gave her a bit of hope. But she was afraid to trust him too much just yet. She needed time to adjust to the new Blake. She sighed. "I haven't been on a picnic in years. And I'm looking forward to it," she confessed with a smile, "even if he only wants me along because Sarah likes me."

"Sarah's a cute little girl." Bess sighed. "Bobby and I are ready to start a family of our own, but I can't seem to get pregnant. Oh, well, it takes time, I guess. Do you want something to eat?"

"I'm too nervous to eat," Meredith said honestly, her eyes still soft with memories of the night before. "I hope I'm wearing the right thing."

Bess studied her. Jeans, sneakers, a white tank top that showed off her pretty tan and emphasized her full, high breasts, and her dark hair loose around her shoulders. "You look great," she said. "And there's no rain in the forecast, so you should be fine."

"I should have slept longer," Meredith wailed. "I'll be a nervous wreck . . . Oh!"

The jangling of the telephone startled her, but Bess only smiled.

"If I were a gambling woman," Bess said as she went to answer it, "I'd bet my egg money that Blake's as nervous and impatient as you are." She picked the receiver up, said hello, then glanced amusedly at Meredith, whose heart was doing a marathon race in her chest. "Yes, she's ready, Blake," she said. "You might as well come get her before she wears out my carpet. I'll tell her. See you."

"How could you say that!" Meredith cried. "My best friend, and you sold me out to the enemy!"

"He isn't the enemy, and I think Blake needs all the advantages he can get." Bess's smile faded. "He's such a lonely man, Meredith. He was infatuated with Nina and he let himself be suckered into marriage without realizing she only wanted his money. He's paid for that mistake enough, don't you think?"

"There are some things you don't know," Meredith said.

"I'm sure there are. But if you love him in spite of those things I don't know, then it's foolish to risk your future out of spite and vengeance."

Meredith smiled wearily. "I don't have the strength for vengeance," she replied. "I wanted to get even for a long time after I left here, but when I saw him again..." She shrugged. "It's just like old times. I can't talk straight or walk without trembling when he gets within a foot of me. I never should have come back. He's going to hurt me again if I give him an opening. After what Nina did to him, he's not going to make it easy for any woman to get close. Least of all me."

"Give it a chance," Bess advised. "Nothing comes to us without some kind of risk. I've learned a lot about compromise since Bobby and I almost split up a few years ago. I've learned that pride is a poor bedfellow."

"I'm glad you two are getting along so well."

"So am I. I went a bit bonkers over my sexy brother-in-law for a while, but Elissa came along and solved all my problems," Bess confessed with a grin. "King Roper has a gunpowder temper, if you remember." Meredith grinned, because she did. "I couldn't stand up to him, but Elissa didn't give an inch. Not that they do much fighting these days, but they had a rocky start."

"She's so sweet," Meredith murmured. "I liked her the minute I met her."

"Most people do. And King would die for her."

Those words kept echoing in Meredith's brain as she sat in the car, with Blake behind the wheel and Sarah chattering away in the back seat. She looked at Blake's taut profile and tried to imagine having him care enough to die for her. It was a forlorn hope that he'd ever love her. His reserved nature and Nina's cruelty wouldn't let him.

He glanced at her and saw that sadness in her eyes. "What is it?" he asked.

"Nothing." She smiled at Sarah, who was looking worried. "I'm just barely awake."

Blake lifted an eyebrow as the powerful car ate up the miles. "That explains why you were up and dressed at eight when I said we'd be at Bess's at nine."

"I couldn't sleep," she muttered.

"Neither could I," he replied. "Sarah was too excited to stay in bed this morning," he added, just when Meredith was breathless at the thought that the memory of the way he'd kissed her had been the reason he didn't sleep.

"I'm so glad you came, Merry," Sarah said, hugging her new Mr. Friend stuffed bear in the back seat. "We'll have lots of fun! Daddy says there's a swing!"

"Several," he returned. "Jack's Corner has added a new park since you were here," he told Meredith. "It has swings and a sandbox and one of those things kids love to climb on. We can sit on a bench and watch her. Then there are plenty of tables. I thought we'd pick up something at one of the fast food stores for lunch, since Amie wasn't around to fix a picnic basket."

"Did she call?"

"Yes. Her sister is recovering very well, but it will be at least two weeks more before Amie comes back."

"How are you managing?"

"Not very well," he confessed. "I'm no cook, and there are things Amie could do for Sarah that I'm not comfortable doing."

"Daddy won't bathe me," Sarah called out. "He says he doesn't know how."

A flush of color worked its way up Blake's cheekbones and Meredith felt the embarrassment with him. It would be hard for a man to do such things for a daughter when he'd rarely been around a woman and never around little girls.

"I could..." Meredith hesitated at his sharp glance and then plowed ahead. "I could bathe her for you tonight. I wouldn't mind."

"Oh, Merry, could you?" Sarah enthused.

"If your father doesn't mind," she continued with a concerned glance in Blake's direction.

"I wouldn't mind," he said, without taking his eyes from the road.

"And you can tell me some more stories, Merry," Sarah said. "I specially like 'The Ugly Ducking.'"

"Duckling," Blake corrected, and he smiled faintly at his child. "I guess that story fits both of us, sprout."

"Neither of you," Meredith interrupted. "You both have character and stubborn wills. That's worth a lot more than beauty."

"Daddy has a scar," Sarah piped up.

Meredith smiled at the child. "A mark of courage," she corrected. "And your father was always handsome enough that it didn't matter."

Blake felt his chest grow two sizes. His gaze darted to Meredith's face and he searched her eyes long and intently. As she was feeling the effect of that glance, he forced his eyes back to the road barely in time to avoid running the car into a ditch.

"Sorry," Meredith murmured with a grimace.

"No need." He turned the car down the street that led to the city park and pulled it into a vacant parking space.

"It's beautiful," Meredith said, looking at the expanse of wooded land with a children's playground and a gazebo. There was even a fountain. At this time of the day, though, the area was fairly deserted. Dew was still on the grass, and as they walked to the benches overlooking the playground, Meredith laughed as her sneakers quickly became soaked.

"Your feet are getting wet," Sarah said, laughing, too. "But I have my cowgirl boots on!"

"I think I can spare your feet," Blake murmured.

Before she realized what he intended, Blake bent and whipped Meredith off the ground, carrying her close to his chest without any sign of strain.

"Gosh, you're strong, Daddy," Sarah remarked.

"He always was," Meredith said involuntarily, and her eyes looked up into Blake's, full of memories, full of helpless vulnerability.

His arms contracted a fraction, but he didn't look at her. He didn't dare. He could already feel the effect that rapt stare had on his body. If he gazed at Meredith's soft, yielding face, he would start kissing her despite the small audience of one watching them so closely.

He put her down on the sidewalk without a word and moved to the bench to sit down, leaning back and crossing one booted foot over his jeans-clad knee. "Well, sit down," he said impatiently. "Sarah, play while you can. This place probably fills up in an hour or so."

"Yes, Daddy!" Sarah said and she ran for the swings. Meredith sat down beside Blake, still glowing and warm from the feel of his arms and savoring the warm, cologne-scented fragrance of his lean body. "She's already a different child," she commented, watching Sarah laugh as she pumped her little legs to make the swing go higher.

"She's less wild," Blake agreed. He took off his hat and put it next to him on the bench, pausing to run his hand through his thick black hair. "But she isn't quite secure yet. The nightmares haven't stopped completely. And I've had less time to spend with her lately. Business goes on. A lot of jobs depend on the decisions I make. I can't throw up my hands and stay home every day.''

"Sarah likes Amie, doesn't she?" Meredith asked.

"Amie won't be here for several weeks, Meredith," he said impatiently. "That's what I'm worried about. Monday morning I've got a board meeting. What do I do with Sarah, take her along?"

"I see your problem." Meredith sighed, fingering the face of her watch. "Well . . . I could keep her for you."

He didn't dare let himself react to that offer, even if it was the second time in a day that she'd volunteered to spend time with Sarah. It wouldn't do to get his hopes up too high.

"Could you?" he asked, and turned his head so that his green eyes pinned her gray ones.

"All I have to do is the autographing," she said. "And that's next Saturday. The rest of my time is vacation."

"You'd need to be at the house," he said with apparent unconcern. He pursed his lips, watching Sarah. "And considering how late I get home some nights, it's hardly worth rousing Bobby and Bess to let you in just for a few hours. Is it?"

She colored. "Blake, I don't care if this is the nineteen eighties, I can't move into your house. . . ."

He glanced at her and saw the rose-red blush. "I won't seduce you. I told you that Wednesday, and I meant it."

The blush deepened. She averted her gaze to Sarah and her heart shook her with its mad beat. "I know you won't go back on your word, Blake," she whispered. "But it's what people would think."

"And you're a famous author," he said, his eyes narrowing. "God forbid that I should tarnish your reputation."

"Don't start on me." She sighed miserably and got up. "This isn't a good idea. I shouldn't have come...!"

He got up, too, and caught her by the waist, holding her in front of him. "I'm sorry," he bit off. "I've never given a damn what people thought, but I guess when you aren't looked down on to begin with, reputations matter."

She looked up at him with soft, compassionate eyes. "I never looked down on you."

His jaw clenched. "Don't you think I know that now?" he asked huskily. He pulled her hand to his chest and smoothed over the neat pink nails, his eyes on her long fingers. "You were always defending me."

"And you hated it," she recalled with a sad smile. "I always seemed to make you mad—"

"I told you," he interrupted. "I wanted you, and I didn't know how to handle it. I knew it was impossible to seduce you, and I'd given my word that I was going to marry Nina." His shoulders lifted and fell. "It wasn't conscious, but afterward when I thought about what I did to you that day, I thought maybe it would be easier for you if I made you hate me." He looked up into her gray eyes with quiet sincerity.

Her face felt hot. She searched his hard expression for a long moment. "I suppose in a way it was," she said finally. "But it undermined my confidence. I couldn't believe any man would want me."

"Which worked to my advantage," he whispered, smiling faintly. "Because you weren't tempted to experiment with anyone else." The smile faded. "You're still a virgin. And your first man, Meredith, is going to be me."

Her heart stopped and then ran wild. "That's the most chauvinistic—"

He stopped her by simply lowering his head until his lips were almost touching hers. She could taste his coffee-flavored breath and the intimacy of it made her knees feel rubbery. "I am chauvinistic," he whispered. "And possessive. And hard as nails. I can't help those traits. Life hasn't been kind to me. Not until just recently."

His hands were on her shoulders, holding her in place, and his eyes were on her mouth in a way that made her breath rustle in her throat.

"Sa-Sarah Jane . . ." she stammered.

"Is facing the opposite direction and doesn't have eyes in the back of her head," he murmured. "So just give me your mouth without a struggle, little one, and I'll show you how gentle I can be when I try."

He felt her mouth accept his with the first touch, felt her body give when he drew her against his hard chest. She sighed into his mouth, and his brows drew together tightly over his closed eyes with the sheer pleasure of holding her.

She reached up under his arms to hold him and her body melted without a vestige of fear. Even when she felt the inevitable effect of her closeness on his powerful body, she didn't flinch or try to move away. He was her heart. Despite the pain and the anguish of years ago, he was all she knew or wanted of love.

His hands smoothed her hair as his hard mouth moved slowly on hers. She'd dreamed of this for so many years, dreamed of his mouth taking hers with exquisite tenderness, giving as much as he took. But the dreams paled beside the sweet reality. Her nails scraped against his back, loving the way the muscles rippled under her fingers.

His mouth lifted a fraction of an inch, and his breath was audible. "Who taught you to do that?" he whispered huskily.

"Nobody. I...guess it comes naturally," she whispered back.

His hands slid up her back to her hair and tangled gently in it. "Your mouth is very soft," he said unsteadily. "And it tastes of coffee and mint."

"I had Irish mocha mint coffee," she said.

"Did you?" He searched her eyes slowly. "Your legs are trembling," he remarked.

She laughed nervously. "I'm not surprised," she confessed. "My knees are wobbly."

He smiled, and the smile echoed in his eyes. "Are they?"

"Daddy, watch how high I can go!" a small voice called out.

Blake reluctantly loosened his hold on Meredith. "I'm watching," he called back.

Sarah Jane was swinging high and laughing. "I can almost touch the sky!" she said.

"Funny, so can I," Blake murmured. He glanced at Meredith, and he wasn't smiling.

She looked back, her heart threatening to burst. He took her hand in his, threading his fingers through hers so that he had them pressed in an almost intimate hold.

"To hell with your reputation," he said huskily. "Move in with us for a couple of weeks. Nobody will know except Bess and Bobby, and they're not judgmental."

She wanted to. Her worried eyes searched his. "Your company is an old and very conservative one. Your board of directors wouldn't like it at all."

"My board of directors doesn't dictate my private life," he replied. "We could sit close on the couch and watch television at night with Sarah. We could have breakfast together in the kitchen. If Sarah had nightmares, she could climb in with you. You could read her stories and I could listen." He smiled crookedly. "I don't remember anybody ever reading me a story, Meredith," he added. "My uncle wasn't the type. I grew up in a world without fairy tales and happy endings. Maybe that's why I'm so bitter. I don't want Sarah to end up like me."

"Don't run yourself down," she said softly. Her eyes searched over his face warmly. "I think you turned out pretty well."

He touched her hair with a big, lean hand. "I never meant to be as cruel to you as I was." He sighed wearily. "And I guess if it hadn't been for Sarah, you wouldn't have come near me again, would you?" he asked.

She lowered her eyes to his chest. "I don't know," she said honestly. "I was still bitter, and a little afraid of you when I came back. But when I saw you with Sarah..." Her eyes lifted. "You might not realize it, but you're different when she's around. She takes some of the rough edges off you."

"She's pretty special. No thanks to Nina," he added curtly. "God knows why she kept the child when she so obviously didn't want her."

"Maybe her husband did."

"If he did, he sure changed his tune when he found out she was mine. He turned his back on her completely. I'm damned if I could have done that to a child," he said coldly. "Whether or not we shared the same blood, there are bonds equally strong."

"Not everyone has a sense of honor," Meredith reminded him. "Your sense of honor was always one of your strongest traits."

"It still is." He sat down on the bench again, tugging her down beside him and drawing her closer while Sarah stopped the swing and ran to the sandbox. "She'll carry half that sand home with us," he murmured ruefully.

"Sand brushes off," Meredith reminded him.

He smiled. "So it does." He leaned back and his hand contracted on her shoulder. "She's crazy about you."

"I like her, too. She's a wonderful little girl."

"I hope you'll still think so after she's treated you to one of her tantrums."

"Most children have those," she reminded him. She leaned back against his arm and looked up at him. Impulsively she reached up and touched the white line of scar tissue on his face, noticing the way he flinched and grabbed her hand. "It's not unsightly," she said softly, and she smiled. "I told Sarah it was a mark of courage, and it is. You got it because of me. It was my fault."

His fingers curled around hers and pressed before he led them back to the scar and let her touch it. "Saving you from a wild bronc," he recalled, smiling because it was a lot like what had happened to Sarah in the corral. "You weren't after a lacy white handkerchief. Instead it was a kitten that had run into the corral. I got to you in the nick of time, but I ran face first into a piece of tin on the way out."

"You used words I'd never heard before or since," she murmured sheepishly. "And I deserved every one of them. But you let me patch you up, anyway. That was sweet," she said unthinkingly, and then lowered her eyes.

" 'Sweet.' " His hard lips pursed as he studied her face. "You'll never know what I felt. The atmosphere was electric that day. I gritted my teeth and forced myself to glare at you. It kept me from doing what I really wanted to do."

"Which was?" she asked, curious, because she remembered too well the cold fury in his face and voice as she'd doctored him.

"I wanted to pull you into my lap and kiss the breath out of you," he said huskily. "You were wearing a cotton blouse with nothing, not a damned thing, under it. I could see the outline of your breasts under the blouse and I wanted to touch them so badly that I shook with longing. It wasn't more than a day later that I did just that, in the stable. You didn't know," he guessed, watching the expressions play across her face.

"No," she admitted breathlessly. "I had no idea. Of course, I was shaking a little myself, and trying so hard to hide my reaction from you that I didn't notice what you might be feeling."

"I lay awake all night, remembering the way you looked and sounded and smelled." He glanced at Sarah, watching her make a pointed castle in the sand and stack twigs around it for doors and windows. "I woke up aching. And then, days later, they read the will, and I went wild. Nina was clinging to me, I was confused about what I felt for you and for her." He shrugged. "I went crazy. That's why I said such cruel things to you. I wanted you so badly. When I saw you later, I couldn't resist one last chance to hold you, to taste you. So I kissed you. It took every last ounce of willpower I had to pull back."

"I really hated you for that," she said, remembering. "I knew you were getting even for the will, for what your uncle tried to do. I never realized that you really wanted me." She smiled self-consciously.

His lips twisted. "Do you think a man can fake desire?" he asked with a level stare.

She flushed and avoided his gaze. "No."

"At least I know now that I'm still capable of feeling it," he said heavily, his eyes going again to Sarah. "It's been a long dry spell. I couldn't bear the thought of having some other woman cut up my pride the way Nina did. And no one knows better than I do that I'm not much good in bed."

"I think that depends on who you're in bed with," she said, staring at his shirt. "When two people care about each other, it's supposed to be magic, even if neither of them has any experience."

"It wasn't magic for us, and we both fit into that category the day the will was read," he murmured softly.

"That's true. But I fought you. I didn't understand what was happening," she confessed.

He studied her down-bent head. "Do you think it might be different now that we've both had five years to mature?"

"I don't know," she said.

His lean hand touched her hair hesitantly and trailed down her cheek to her soft mouth. "I haven't learned a lot," he said, his voice quiet and deep. He drew in a slow breath. "And you knock me off balance pretty bad. I might frighten you if things got out of hand."

He sounded as if the thought tormented him. She lifted her eyes and looked up at him. "Oh, no," she said softly. "You wouldn't hurt me."

His heart stampeded in his chest when she looked at him that way. "Would you go that far with me?" he whispered.

She couldn't sustain that piercing green-eyed gaze. Her eyes fell to his hard mouth. "Don't ask me, Blake," she pleaded. "I would, but I'd hate both of us. All those years of strict upbringing don't just go away because we want them to. I'm not made for a permissive life. Not even with you."

She made it sound as if he were the exception to the rule, and he felt a sting of pure unadulterated masculine pride at her words. She wanted to. He smiled slowly. That made things a little easier. Of course, the walls were all still up. The smile faded when he realized that those scruples of hers were going to stop him, because his own conscience and sense of honor wouldn't let him seduce her. Not even if she wanted him to.

"I guess I'm not either, if you want the truth." He sighed. "You and I are a dying breed, honey."

She heard the endearment with a sense of awe. It was the first time he'd used one with her, the very first time. She was aware of a new warmth deep inside her as she savored it in her mind.

"Daddy, look at my sand castle!" Sarah Jane called. "Isn't it pretty? But I'm hungry. And I want to go to the bathroom."

Blake smiled involuntarily. "Okay, sprout. Come on." He moved slightly away from Meredith. "She doesn't settle for long. Her mind is like a grasshopper."

"I think it's the age." Meredith smiled. She knelt and held out her arms for Sarah to run into, and she lifted the child, hugging her close. "You smell nice," she said. "What do you have on?"

"It's Daddy's," Sarah said, and Blake's eyebrows shot up. "It was on his table and I got me some. Isn't it nice? Daddy always smells good."

"Yes, he does." Meredith was fighting a losing battle with the giggles. She looked at Blake's astounded face and burst out laughing.

"So that's where it went," he murmured, sniffing Sarah and wrinkling his nose. "Sprout, that stuff's for me. It's not for little girls."

"I want to be like you, Daddy," Sarah said simply, and there was the sweetest, warmest light in her green yees.

Blake smiled at her fully for the first time, his white teeth flashing against his dark tan. "Well, well. I guess I'll have to teach you how to ride and rope, then."

"Oh, yes!" Sarah agreed. "I can ride a horse now. And I can rope anything. Can't I, Merry?"

Meredith almost agreed, but Blake's eyes were making veiled threats.

"You'd better wait a bit, until your daddy can teach you properly," Meredith said carefully, and Blake nodded in approval.

"I hate to wait," Sarah muttered.

"Don't we all," Blake murmured, but he didn't look at Meredith as he started toward the car. "Let's find someplace that sells food."

They found a small convenience store with rest rooms just a little way down the road, where they bought coffee and soft drinks and the fixings for sandwiches, along with pickles and chips. Blake drove them back to the park, which was beginning to fill up.

"I know a better place than this," he remarked. "Sarah, how would you like to wade in the river?"

"Oh, boy!" she exclaimed.

He smiled at Meredith, who smiled back. "Then let's go. We're between the Canadian and the North Canadian rivers. Take your pick."

"The North Canadian, then," Meredith said.

He turned the car and shot off in the opposite direction, while Sarah Jane asked a hundred questions about

Oklahoma, the rivers, the Indians and why the sky was blue.

Meredith just sat quietly beside Blake as he drove, admiring his lean hands on the wheel, the ease with which he maneuvered through Jack's Corner and out onto the plains. He didn't try to talk while he drove, which was good, because Sarah wouldn't have let him get a word in edgewise, anyway.

Sarah's chatter gave Meredith a breathing space and she used it to worry over Blake's unexpected proposal. He wanted her to move in with him and Sarah, and she was more tempted than he knew. She had to keep reminding herself that she had a lot to lose—and it was more than just a question of her reputation and his. It was a question of her own will and whether she could trust herself to say no to Blake if he decided to turn on the heat.

He wasn't a terribly experienced man, but that wouldn't matter if he started kissing her. She still loved him. If he wanted her, she wasn't sure that all her scruples would keep her out of his bed.

And being the old-fashioned man he was, she didn't know what would happen if she gave in. He'd probably feel obliged to offer to marry her. That would ruin everything. She didn't want a marriage based on obligation. If he grew to care about her, and wanted her for his own sake and not Sarah's . . .

She forced her mind back to the present. It didn't do to anticipate fate. Regardless of how she felt, it was Blake's feelings that mattered now. He had to want more than just her body before she could feel comfortable about the future.

Seven

Blake drove over the bridge that straddled the Canadian River, but he didn't stop on its banks. He kept driving until finally he turned off on a dirt road and they went still another short distance. He stopped the car under an oak tree and helped Meredith and Sarah Jane out into the shade.

"Where are we?" Meredith asked, disoriented.

He smiled. "Come and see." He took Sarah's hand and led them through the trees to a huge body of water. "Know where you are now?" he asked.

Meredith laughed. "Lake Thunderbird!" she burst out. "But this isn't the way to get to it! And this isn't the North Canadian or the Canadian. It's in between!"

"Don't confuse the issue with a lot of facts," he said with dry humor. "Isn't this a nice place for a picnic?" he went on. "We have shade and peace and quiet."

"Who owns this land?"

He pursed his lips. "Well, actually, it's part of what I inherited from my uncle. It's only fifteen acres, but I like it here." He looked around the wooded area with eyes that appreciated its natural beauty. "When I need to think out something, I come here. I guess that's why I've never built on it. I like it this way."

"Yes, I can see why," Meredith agreed. Birds were singing nearby, and the wind brushed leafy branches together with soft whispers of sound. She closed her eyes and let the breeze lift her hair, and she thought that with Sarah and Blake beside her, she'd never been closer to heaven.

"Sarah, don't go too near the edge," Blake cautioned.

"But you said I could go wading," the child protested, and began to look mutinous.

"So I did," he agreed. "But not here. After we eat, there's a nice place farther down the road where you can wade. Okay?"

For several long seconds, she matched her small will against his. But in the end she gave in. "Okay," she said.

Blake got out the cold cuts and bread, and a heavy cloth to spread on the grass. They ate in contented silence as Sarah offered crumbs to ants and other insects, fascinated with the variety of tiny life.

"Haven't you ever seen a bug before, Sarah?" Meredith asked.

"Not really," the little girl replied. "Mama said they're nasty and she killed them. But the man on TV says that bugs are bene... bene..."

"Beneficial," Blake said. "And I could argue that with the man on TV, especially when they get into the hides of my cattle."

Meredith smiled at him. He smiled back. Then the smiles faded and they were looking at each other openly, with a blistering kind of attraction that made Meredith's body go hot. She'd never experienced that electricity with anyone except Blake. Probably she never would, but she had to get a grip on herself before it was too late.

She forced her eyes down to the cloth. "How about another sandwich?" she offered with forced cheer.

After they finished the makeshift meal, Blake drove them down to the small stream. It ran across the dirt road, and Sarah tugged off her cowgirl boots in a fever to get to the clear, rippling water. Butterflies drifted down on the wet sand, and Blake smiled at the picture the child made walking barefoot through the water.

"I used to do that when I was a boy," Blake said, hands in his pockets as he leaned against the trunk of the car and watched her. "Kids who live in cities miss a hell of a lot."

"Yes, they do. I can remember playing like this, too. We used to get water from streams occasionally in oil drums, when the well went dry." Her eyes had a wistful, faraway look. "We were so poor in those days. I never realized how poor until I went to a birthday party in grammar school and saw how other kids lived." She sighed. "I never told my parents how devastating it was. But I realized then what a difference money makes."

"It doesn't seem to have changed you all that much, Meredith," he said, studying her quietly. "You're a little more confident than you used to be, but you're no snob."

"Thank you." She twisted the small gold-braid ring on her finger nervously. "But I'm not in your class yet. I get by and that's all."

"A Porsche convertible is more than just getting by," he mused.

"I felt reckless the day I bought it. I was thinking about coming back here and facing the past," she confessed. "I bought it to give me confidence."

"We all need confidence boosters from time to time," Blake replied quietly, his eyes on Sarah. "She's slowly coming out of the past. I like seeing her laugh. She didn't in those first few days with me."

"I guess she was afraid to," Meredith said. "She hasn't really had much security in her young life."

"She's got it now. As long as I live, I'll take care of her."

The pride and faint possessiveness in his deep voice touched Meredith. She wondered how it would feel to have him say the same thing about her, and she blushed. Blake might allow himself to become vulnerable with a small child, but she had serious doubts about his ability to really love a woman. Nina had hurt him too badly.

They stayed another few minutes, and then Sarah announced that she needed to find a bathroom again. With an amused smile, Blake loaded them into the car and set out for a gas station.

They drove around looking at the countryside until almost dark. Then they went home and Meredith helped Sarah get a bath. After that, she settled down by the child's bedside to tell her some stories before she fell asleep.

She was halfway through "Sleeping Beauty," when Blake came into the room and sat down, legs crossed, in the chair by the window to listen. He was a little intimidating, but Sarah laughed and encouraged Meredith, and in no time she was lost in the fantasy herself.

She told the child two more stories and Sarah's eyelids grew heavier by the second. By the time Meredith had started on "Snow White," Sarah Jane was sound asleep.

Meredith got up, tucked the covers around the tired little body and bent impulsively to kiss Sarah good-night.

"That's another thing she's missed," Blake remarked as he joined her by the bed. "Being kissed good-night." He shifted, his hands in his pockets as he looked down at his daughter. "Showing affection is difficult for me." He glanced at Meredith. "My uncle wasn't the kissing sort." He smiled a little. "And I guess you know that."

She laughed. "Yes. I remember. He was a sweet man, but he hated touching or being touched."

"So do I," Blake replied. His eyes slid over Meredith's soft oval face. "Except by you," he added quietly. "I used to love to get cut up when you were here because you always patched me up. I loved the feel of your hands on my skin. I remember how soft and caring they were." He sighed heavily and turned away. "We'd better get out of here before we wake her up."

It was obviously embarrassing to him to admit how much he'd enjoyed her doctoring. That was surprising. She hadn't realized until he'd said it just how many minor accidents he seemed to have had in the old days, when she was around. She smiled to herself. That was one more tiny secret to cherish in the years ahead, when these sweet days were just a memory and Blake was far out of her reach.

"Why are you smiling?" he asked curtly.

She looked across at him as she closed Sarah's door. "I was thinking how ironic it is. I loved it when you needed patching up because it gave me an excuse to get close to you." She colored a little as she averted her eyes.

"Isn't it amazing how green we both were?" he asked. "Considering our ages. We weren't kids."

"No."

The atmosphere was getting tenser by the second. She could almost feel the hard pressure of his mouth on her lips, and the way he was watching her, with that single-minded level stare, made her knees feel weak under her.

"How do you remember all those fairy tales?" Blake asked to relieve the tension that he was feeling.

"I don't know. It's a knack, I guess. Blake, you really do need to get her some storybooks," she said.

"You'll have to pick them out," he replied. "I don't know beans about what kids her age read."

"All right. I'll see if Mrs. Donaldson has any in her shop. I noticed some books in the back, but I didn't take time to look at them."

"I appreciate your help tonight," he said. "Some facets of being a parent are difficult. Especially dealing with frilly underwear and baths." He leaned against the wall, in no hurry to go downstairs, and his green eyes wandered slowly over Meredith's exquisite figure in the revealing button-up white tank top and well-fitting blue jeans. His eyes narrowed on that top because he didn't think there was anything under it and her breasts were hard tipped when they hadn't been a minute ago. "You're very maternal."

"I like children. Shouldn't we go downstairs?" she added nervously, because she felt the impact of his eyes on her breasts.

"Why? Do you suspect that I'm going to drag you into my bedroom and lock the door?"

"Of course not," she said too quickly.

"Pity," he remarked, shouldering away from the wall. "Because that's exactly what I'm going to do."

And he did, quickly, smoothly and with deadly efficiency. Before Meredith had time to say anything, he had her in his room. He paused to lock the door and then lowered her onto the middle of the king-size bed.

She lay there breathless, staring up at him, as he bent over her, one lean hand on either side of her head, his green eyes biting into hers.

"How afraid of me are you, Meredith?" he asked quietly. "If I start making love to you, are you going to kick and scream for help?"

Her lips parted as she looked up at him. She wasn't afraid of him at all. During the day, something had happened to both of them. The time they'd spent together had acted to bring them close. She knew more about him now than she ever had, and the thought uppermost in her mind was how much she loved him. Her eyes fell to his hard mouth, and she wanted it, and him, almost shockingly.

"No, I'm not frightened," she said. "Because I know you won't hurt me or force me to do anything I don't want to. You said so."

He seemed to relax a little. "That's true. I meant it, too." His eyes slid down her body, lingering on the thrust of her breasts against the tank top and the way her jeans clung to her rounded hips and long legs. "You can't imagine the effect you've had on me all day in that getup. Do you know how sexy you are?"

"Me?" she asked with a faint, delighted smile.

"You." He lifted his gaze back to collide with hers. "And you aren't getting out of here yet."

She felt tiny tremors shooting up and down her spine at the delicious threat. "I'm not?" she asked huskily.

He lowered himself down over her so that his chest was almost touching her breasts and his mouth was within an inch of hers. "No," he breathed. "You're not."

Her hands slid up around his neck and her eyes dropped to his mouth. He smelled of cologne and she loved the feel of his shoulders and back under her hands, the hard muscles under the thin shirt. Her breath jerked out of her throat as she felt the warm threat of his body and tasted his coffee-scented breath on her lips.

"Just relax," he whispered as his mouth brushed hers. "I won't hurt you."

Her hands slid into his thick hair and she let her body sink under the warm weight of his chest as it pressed against hers. His mouth was slow and hungry, and she didn't mind when it began to probe inside her own. She'd never kissed anyone except Blake this way, and she loved the sensuality of it. She let his tongue enter her mouth and her hands clung as the new sensations ran like fire along her nerves and made her weak.

She kissed him back, savoring the warm hungry mouth on hers. One of his hands supported her neck, but the other slid over her shoulder and suddenly covered her soft breast.

She took an audible breath and he lifted his head, but he didn't remove his hand.

"You're a woman now," he whispered. "And we've done this together once before. Except that this time, I'm not so green."

"Yes." She touched his fingers, lightly brushing them, while her eyes looked into his glittering ones with building excitement. Her swollen lips parted. "You could... unbutton it," she whispered shakily. "I'm not wearing anything under it."

She colored as she said it, and he realized how much courage it took for her to make him such an offer. Was she trying to prove that she trusted him, or could she feel the same hunger he did?

His fingers slid to the buttons and slowly began to slip them out of the buttonholes. And all the while, he searched her eyes, held them. "Why aren't you wearing anything underneath?" he asked when he'd finished and the edges were still touching.

"Don't you know, Blake?" she whispered with aching hunger. She arched just a fraction of an inch.

The invitation was as blatant as if she'd shouted it. He slowly peeled the edges of the tank top away from her full, firm breasts and let his eyes fall to them. They were as beautiful as they had been five years ago. A little fuller now, firmer. The color of seashells and rose petals, he thought dizzily as his eyes lingered on the hard tips that signaled her desire.

"Have you ever let any other man see you like this?" he whispered, because it was suddenly important.

"Only you," she replied, and her eyes were warm and soft, almost loving as they met his. "How could I let anyone else...?" she asked huskily.

"Meredith, you're exquisite," he bit off. His fingers brushed over one perfect breast lightly, barely touching it, and she cried out.

The sound startled him. He stopped at once, scowling at her in open concern. "Did I hurt you?" he asked softly. "I knew you were delicate there. I didn't mean to be rough with you."

She stared at him curiously, biting her lower lip as she tried to control the tremors he'd set off. "Blake...it didn't hurt," she said hesitantly.

"You cried out," he said, his eyes steady and honestly worried.

She colored furiously. "Yes."

The scowl stayed as his hand moved again. His green eyes held hers the whole time while he stroked her gently, smoothed the hard tip between his fingers and cupped her in his lean, rough hand. And she whimpered softly and cried out again, her body shivering and lifting up to him.

"Damn Nina!" he whispered roughly.

Meredith was too drugged to understand what he'd said at first. Her whirling thoughts barely registered in her mind. "What?"

"Never mind," he whispered huskily. "Oh, God, Meredith . . . !" His mouth went down against her breast, and she moaned, arching under him. The sound and her trembling drove him crazy.

He kissed every soft inch of her above her hips, savoring both breasts, nibbling at her creamy skin, dragging the edge of his teeth with exquisite tenderness over her stomach and rib cage. And all the while his hands caressed her, adored her. He made a meal of her, and long before he lifted his head, she was crying and pleading with him for something more than he was giving her.

He dragged air into his lungs, his eyes wild, his chest rising and falling raggedly as he looked down into her abandoned eyes.

Her face fascinated him. She looked as if he was torturing her, but her hands were pulling at his head, her soft voice was begging for his mouth. She moaned, but not in pain. And the most exquisite sensations racked his lean body as he poised over her. "You want me," he whispered huskily.

"Yes."

"Badly," he continued.

"Yes!"

His hands smoothed over her breasts and she shuddered. His breath caught. "I never dreamed a woman could sound like that. I never knew . . ." He bent to her mouth and kissed it softly. "My God, she was suffering me, and I didn't even have the experience to realize it."

"What?"

He dragged himself into a sitting position, and when she made a halfhearted effort to cover herself he pulled her wrist away. "Don't do that," he said quietly. "You're the most beautiful thing I've ever seen in my life. I won't hurt you."

"I know that. I'm just...embarrassed," she faltered, flushing.

"You shouldn't be," he said firmly. "The first intimacy I ever shared with a woman was with you. And your first one was with me. I know what you look like. I've seen you every night in my dreams."

She relaxed a little, sighing as she sank back on the bed. "It's just new," she tried to explain.

"Yes, I know." He brushed his fingertips over a firm breast and watched her shiver with pleasure. "That's sweet," he breathed. "That's so damned sweet, Meredith."

Her breath sighed out. "Blake..."

"What do you want?" he asked, reading the hesitant curiosity in her eyes. "Tell me. I'll do anything you want."

"Could you...unbutton your shirt and let me look at you?" she whispered.

His blood surged in his veins. He flicked buttons open with a hand that was deftly efficient even as he trembled inside with the hunger she aroused. He moved the fabric aside, and when he saw the sheer delight in her eyes at the thick mat of hair over impressive muscle, arrowing down to his jeans, he stripped the whole damned shirt off and threw it on the floor to give her an unobstructed view.

She held out her arms, and he groaned as he went into them, shuddering when he felt her nipples press against his chest as he crushed her into the mattress.

"Blake," she moaned. Her arms clung and her lips searched blindly for his. She found them and kissed him with all her heart, feeling his mouth tremble as it increased its hungry pressure.

He slid over her. His hands found her hips and urged them up against his, moving them against his rhythmically, letting her experience the full surge of his arousal.

She was whimpering, and he felt his control giving. It would only take another few seconds...

"No!" he bit off. He jerked himself away from her and rolled over, but he couldn't get to his feet. He lay there doubled up, while Meredith managed to get her trembling arms to support her. But she didn't touch him. He was shivering and she wanted to cry because she knew it was hurting him that he'd had to stop.

"I'm sorry," she wept. "It's all my fault."

"No, it isn't," he said through his teeth. He drew in sharp breaths until he could get himself under control. His body relaxed and he lay there for a long moment, fighting the need to roll over and strip her and submerge himself in her soft warm body.

"I wouldn't have stopped you," she breathed.

"I know that, too." He finally dragged himself up and ran his hands through his damp hair. His eyes darted to her half-clad body, softening as they swept over her full breasts. "Button your top," he said gently. "Or I'm going to start screaming my head off."

She managed a shaky smile as she pulled her top together and buttoned it with trembling fingers. "You make me feel beautiful," she whispered.

"My God, you are," he returned. His darkened green eyes held hers. "I can't begin to tell you what those sweet little noises you were making did for my ego. I didn't know women made noise or looked like that when they made love."

She searched his eyes. "I don't understand."

"Meredith," he began heavily, "Nina smiled. All through it, all the time. She smiled."

It took a minute for that to get through to her. When it did, she went scarlet. "Oh!"

"I hurt you, that first time," he continued. "So I didn't get any passionate response. I didn't have any other experience when I married Nina, so I thought women were supposed to smile." A corner of his hard mouth lifted ruefully. "But now I know, don't I?"

Her face felt as if she might fry eggs on it. "I couldn't help it," she confessed self-consciously. "I never dreamed there was such pleasure in being touched by a man."

He caught one of her hands and pressed its soft palm hungrily to his mouth. "The pleasure was mutual," he said, his glittering gaze holding hers. "I almost lost it. You let me hold your hips against mine, and I went crazy."

"I'm sorry," she said softly. "I should have pulled away."

"Are you supposed to be superhuman?" he asked reasonably. "I couldn't stop, either. Together we start fires. I wanted nothing more in life than to feel you under me and around me, skin on skin, mouth on mouth, absorbing me into you."

She caught her breath and trembled at the words, seeing the quiet pride in his eyes when he realized the effect they had on her.

"I want to make love to you," he whispered roughly. "Here. Now. On my bed."

"I can't." She closed her eyes. "Please don't ask me."

"It isn't lack of desire. What, then? Scruples?"

She nodded miserably. "You know how I was raised, Blake. It's hard to forget the teachings of a lifetime overnight, even when you want someone very, very much."

"Then suppose you marry me, Meredith."

Her eyes opened wide. "What?"

"We get along well together. You like Sarah. You want me. You've got a career, so I know you don't need my money, and you know I don't need yours. We could build a good life together." He searched her shocked face. "I know I'm not the best matrimonial prospect going. I'm short-tempered and impatient, and I can be ruthless. But you know the worst of me already. There won't be any terrible surprises after the vows."

"I don't know..." she argued.

"You want hearts and flowers and bells ringing." He nodded. "Well, that doesn't always happen. Sometimes you have to settle for practicalities. Tell me you don't want to live with me, Meredith," he challenged with a faintly mocking smile.

"That would be a lie," she said, sighing, "so I won't bother. Yes, I want to live with you. And I'm very fond of Sarah Jane. Taking care of her wouldn't be any trial to me. But you're still not going to let your emotions get in the way of a good business deal, are you, Blake?" she returned. "You want me, but that's all you have to offer."

"For a man, lovemaking is one big part of a relationship," he said, choosing his words. "I don't know much about love. I've never had any." He lifted his eyes back to hers. "If it can be taught, you can teach me. I've never been in love, so you've got a good shot at it already."

She sighed at his summing-up of the situation, despite the ache in her heart for something he might never be able to give her. He was locked up emotionally, and nobody had a key.

He leaned down, his face poised just above hers. "Stop thinking, Meredith," he whispered. His mouth nibbled at her lower lip, smoothing over its delicate swell. His hands cupped her breasts, hot even through the fabric of her tank top and sensual as they caressed her. One long leg insinuated itself between both of hers and she felt it begin to move lazily.

"This isn't fair," she whispered shakily.

"I know. Unbutton your top again," he whispered, and proceeded to tell her exactly why he wanted her to and what he intended to do when she unfastened it.

Her body tingled with heat. She wanted him. Her moan was pure surrender, and he knew it. His heart leaped as he felt her fingers working at the buttons. And then she was all silky warmth under him, her breasts soft and yielding under his searching hands, his hungry mouth.

"You aren't...going to stop...this time, are you?" she whimpered as his mouth grew even bolder.

"That depends on you," he said in a strange, thick tone. "I'd never force you."

"I know." Her mind tumbled while she tried to decide what to do. Part of her knew it was a mistake. But it had been so many years, and she'd done little else but dream of him, of lying in his arms and loving him.

His hand slid to the fastening of her jeans and he lifted himself so that he could see her eyes. "If I start this, I'll have to finish it," he said gently. "I'll go all the way. You have to decide."

Her fingers lingered on his. "I don't know," she moaned. "Blake, I'm afraid. It's going to hurt...!"

"Only a little," he whispered solemnly. "I'll be as slow and tender as I can. I'll do anything you want me to do to make it easier for you." He bent to her mouth, touching it lightly with his. "Meredith, don't you want to know all the secrets?" he asked huskily. "Don't you want to see how much pleasure we can give each other? My God, just kissing you makes my blood run like fire. Having you..." He groaned as he kissed her. "Having you...would be unbearably sweet."

"For me, too." Her arms tightened around his neck, and she buried her face in his hair-roughened chest, savoring the smell and feel of him in her arms.

His hands smoothed down her hips and his weight settled over her, gently, so that he wouldn't frighten her. His mouth trembled as it found hers, and he kissed her with exquisite warmth and tenderness.

"This is how much I want you," he whispered as he moved sensuously against her.

She felt his need, and an answering hunger made her tremble. "Blake...what about...precautions?" she choked out. "I don't know how."

His lips lifted just above hers. "I'm going to marry you," he told her roughly. "But if precautions are important to you, I can use something."

Heat shot through her. She felt her nails digging into his back, heard her own wild cry as she lifted to him. His face hardened and she saw his eyes darken as his mouth came slowly back down to cover hers.

"We should..." she whimpered.

"Yes," he whispered. But his mouth grew demanding, and his last sane thought was that creating babies with Meredith was as natural as wading in country streams and walking in the park. He closed his eyes, shaking with the need to join his aching body to hers and give her the same sweet pleasure he felt when he touched her.

Eight

Meredith trembled, half blind with pleasure as Blake's mouth became more demanding. It was almost enough just to kiss him, to feel the exquisite weight of his body on hers as his hand worked at the fastenings of her clothes.

"The light," she whispered huskily.

He touched her mouth tenderly. "I know," he said deeply, reaching for it. "You might not believe it, little one, but I've got more hang-ups than you have."

The room was in darkness then, except for the faint moonlight seeping in through the white curtains. His hands smoothed down her breasts, savoring their warm fullness. She gasped and he searched for her mouth in the darkness.

"Meredith," he whispered huskily.

"What?" she breathed.

"One of us needs to do something if you don't want me to make you pregnant. You haven't really answered me."

She felt the heat in her cheeks. He was right, it was something they had to consider. She swallowed. "I'm not on the pill," she confessed.

"Do you want me to take care of it?"

Her fingers touched his face, involuntarily running down the scar, while visions of his son in her arms made her tremble with hunger. "I . . . I don't mind, either way," she said unsteadily.

"God!" He buried his face in her throat and shuddered. It was so profound to hear her say that. It would be all of heaven to see her grow big with his child, to share the sweetness of raising it.

"Blake?" she whispered, uncertain.

"I don't mind, either," he said roughly. "Come here."

He pulled her closer still and she melted against him with blinding hope as he began to tease her breasts with his hands. He trailed his fingers around the outer edges, feeling the tension in her body, the heat of her skin as he drew his caresses out, making her wait, building the need, until she caught his wrists and tried to make him touch her.

And he did, finally, so that it was like a tiny fulfillment, and she shuddered and arched into his warm, lean hands. He liked her reactions, delighted in her responses. She had to care about him, he thought dizzily as his hands smoothed away her clothing, to let him do these things to her and to feel such pleasure when he did.

He was slow. Deliberately slow. More patient than he'd ever dreamed of being. He loved the soft sounds that came whispering out of her throat, the way her hands were clinging to him. He loved the very texture of her skin, the sound of her quick breathing like a rustle in the darkness as he touched her more intimately.

He should be out of his mind with the need to have her, he thought in the back of his mind. But stronger than pas-

sion was the need for her to feel the same exquisite sensations that were rippling through his powerful body and
making him tremble with each new touch, each soft kiss.
He wanted much, much more than quick fulfillment. He
wanted to touch all that was Meredith, to join his body to
hers and feel the oneness that he'd read was possible between two people who cared for each other.

His lips smoothed over hers, barely touching, while his
hands found her where she was untouched and gently,
tenderly probed. She gasped under his mouth. Thank God
for books, he thought while he could. He hadn't known
anything about virgins until he'd done some reading the
other night.

"It's all right," he whispered tenderly. "I'm going to be
very gentle, Meredith. I just want to make sure that what
we do won't be any more painful than it has to be."

"I don't mind," she told him softly, clinging.
"Blake...I'd give you anything...!"

"Yes." His mouth whispered against hers. "I'd give you
anything, too, Meredith. I'd do anything to please you,
even forgo my own pleasure."

That didn't sound like lust. Neither did the exquisitely
slow movements of his hands, the gentle crush of his body.
He was hungry, she could feel his need, but he wouldn't
take his pleasure at her expense. That consideration, incredible given the length of abstinence for him, made her
want to cry. He had to care a little to be so...!

Her mind went crazy as his hand moved and she felt a
stab of pleasure so sweet that it lifted her and she cried out.

She clung to him, telling him without words that it was
pleasure, not pain, she was feeling. He warmed, remembering his own earlier withdrawal when she moaned or
gasped, because he'd never known how a woman re-
sponded when giving herself to pleasure.

He opened his mouth on hers and let his tongue gently stab inside her lips, aching at the implied intimacy, delighting in the way her soft, slender body turned in his hands when he did that. She was loving this, he thought dizzily. Loving every second of it, reveling in his mouth, his touch. He could feel her pleasure even as his built and built until he couldn't contain it any longer.

She was trembling now, and tiny whispers of excitement were moaning past her lips as she lay waiting for him, her body twisting sensually with mindless abandon.

He was heady with pride at his own latent abilities. He hadn't dreamed that with his inexperience he could bring her to this frenzy.

He stripped with quick, deft movements and slid onto the coverlet beside her, his hands moving on her body, holding her while he kissed her with whispery tenderness.

"Pl...ease." She managed the one word, and her voice broke on it.

"I want you, too, little one," he breathed against her mouth. "I want you so much."

He balanced his weight on his forearms and slid over her, trembling at the soft warmth of her legs tangling with his. She moved, helping him, and he let his hips ease down.

She felt the first hesitant probing and shuddered, but she didn't tense. She forced her body to relax, not to fight him.

He could feel that, and his mouth smoothed over her lips in silent reassurance.

His hands went to her face, holding it while he kissed her, and he felt her soft cry go into his mouth as he pushed gently against the veil of her womanhood.

And it was easy then. He felt the faint tension go out of her body, felt her sigh feather against his lips.

"I won't ever have to hurt you again," he murmured unsteadily. "I'm sorry it has to be this way for a virgin."

"But it wasn't bad," she whispered back. Her fingers slid into his cool, thick hair. "Oh, Blake..." she whimpered. She kissed him softly. "Blake, it's...incredible!"

"Yes." He touched her eyes, closing them; he touched her nose, cheeks and forehead with lips that were breathlessly tender. And all the while his body moved with equal tenderness, drowning her in the exquisite sensation of oneness. She pulled his mouth to hers as his movements began to lengthen and deepen with shuddering pleasure, her breath filling him, her tiny cries making him feverish with contained passion.

His hands slid under her, savoring the warm, soft skin of her back and hips, holding her to him.

"Meredith—" His voice broke on her name. His eyes closed. He felt the tension growing in his powerful body with each torturously slow movement, felt the control he had beginning to slip. But her control was going, too. She was trembling, clinging, her mouth ardent and hungry. He lifted her up and overwhelmed her with desperate tenderness, and when the spasms came, they were white hot, blinding, but with a gentleness that he couldn't have imagined.

She bit him in her passion, but he was riding waves of completion and he hardly felt her teeth. His hands contracted. He cried her name against her damp throat and the tide washed over him in pulsating shudders.

He heard her crying an eternity later and he managed to lift his head and search her face. "Meredith?" he whispered huskily. "Oh, God, I didn't hurt you, did I?"

"No!" She buried her face against his chest, kissing him there, kissing his throat, his face, everywhere she could reach, with lips that worshipped him. "Blake!" she moaned, her arms contracting around his neck. "Blake...!" She shuddered again and again, and when he realized why, he put his mouth gently against hers and began to move.

The second time was every bit as sweet, but slower, more achingly drawn out. He hadn't dreamed a man could hold out as long as he was managing to. But he adored her with his mouth, his hands, and finally, when she was crying with the tension he'd aroused, he adored her with the slow, worshipping motion of his body in one long, sweet pinnacle of fulfillment.

She couldn't seem to stop crying. She lay in his arms with her wet face pillowed on his chest where the thick hair was damp with sweat. She couldn't let go of him, either, and he seemed to understand that, because he held her even closer and gently brushed her hair away from her face while he kissed her tenderly and soothed her.

"I thought ... passion was uncontrollable and ... and quick ... and men couldn't ... men were rough," she told him.

"How could I be rough with you?" His mouth touched hers, brushing softly over her trembling lips. "Or make something that beautiful into raw sex?"

Her breath sighed out, making little chills against his damp skin. "I'm so glad I waited for you," she said simply, shaken by the experience. "I'm so glad I didn't give in to some man I didn't even like out of curiosity or because everybody else was doing it." She nuzzled her face against him. "You are so wonderful."

He drew her mouth up to his and kissed her possessively. "So are you," he whispered. "I didn't know what lovemaking was until tonight. I didn't know that there could be such pleasure in it," he murmured against her mouth.

"I thought men felt the pleasure with anyone," she replied.

"Apparently it's an individual thing," he said quietly. "Because I never felt anything approaching this before." He heard the words without realizing their importance, until it suddenly came to him that he'd hardly felt anything with Nina. But Meredith's soft young body had sent him spinning into oblivion and he'd done things with her and to her that had come naturally. Perhaps it was instinct. But what if it was something stronger?

He'd called it lovemaking, and it had been. Not sex, or the satisfaction of a need. And he couldn't imagine doing that with anyone except Meredith. Not that way. Not with such staggering tenderness. He hadn't even known he was capable of it.

"I wasn't sure I could wait for you," he confessed, nuzzling her face. "Was it enough?"

Her body burned with the memory, and she kissed his throat with breathless tenderness. "Yes. And…was it for you?" she asked, worried.

"Yes." Only the one word, but there was a wealth of unspoken pleasure in it.

She was beginning to feel self-conscious, and he seemed distant all of a sudden, as if he were withdrawing. Had he satisfied his hunger for her and now he was looking for a way out of what could become an embarrassing situation? Did he regret what they'd done? He had old-fashioned ideas about sex, after all. In fact, so did she, but they hadn't helped once he'd started kissing her. Her love for him had betrayed her into his bed.

"Blake, you don't…I mean, you don't think I'm easy…?" she asked suddenly.

"My God!" he exclaimed. He reached over and turned on the light, blinding her with stark illumination and embarrassment.

She fumbled for the cover, scarlet faced, but he stayed her hand.

"No," he said quietly, his eyes as solemn as his face. "Look at me, Meredith. Let me look at you."

Her eyes darted over him and she looked away quickly as the heat grew in her face, but he turned her eyes back gently.

"I'm not a monster," he said softly. "I'm just a man. Flesh and blood, like you. There's nothing to be frightened of."

She managed not to look away this time, and after the first shock, she found him beautiful, in a very masculine sense. He was looking, too, his eyes reconciling sweet memories of her five years ago with the reality of today.

"You've blossomed," he said after a minute, and there was no masculine mockery or teasing in his tone. It was deep and soft as he searched over her swollen breasts, her flat stomach, the curve of her hips, the elegant sweep of her long legs. "You're much more pleasing to my eyes than the Venus, Meredith," he said huskily. "The sight of you knocks the breath right out of me."

Her breath caught at the emotion in his voice. "You make it sound so natural," she said with faint curiosity.

"Isn't it?" he asked. His green eyes searched her soft gray ones. "We made love. I know your body as well as I know my own. We touched in more than just the conventional way, and you're part of me now. Isn't it natural that I should want to see the lovely body I've known so intimately?"

She colored, but she smiled. "Yes."

"And to answer your other question, Meredith, no, I don't think you're easy." He smoothed back her dark hair and his eyes slid over her face. "We both knew it wasn't going to be a casual encounter. I knew you were a virgin."

He brought her hand to his lips and kissed the palm tenderly. "We're going to get married and spend the rest of our lives together. That's the only reason I didn't pull away from you. If sex had been all I wanted, I could have had it long before now, and I wouldn't have seduced you in cold blood for my own pleasure."

She searched his darkened eyes. "It isn't just because of Sarah that you want to marry me, is it? Or just because you wanted me—"

He stopped the words with his mouth. "You talk too much. And worry too much. I want to marry you." He lifted his head. "Don't you want to marry me?"

Her eyes softened. "Oh, yes."

"Then stop brooding." He got up, stretching lazily while she watched him with shy fascination. He dug in his chest of drawers and pulled out a set of navy silk pajamas. He tugged the bottoms up over his hard-muscled legs and snapped them before he carried the pajama top to the bed, lifted Meredith into a sitting position and eased her arms into the sleeves.

"It's economical to share these," he murmured dryly when her eyes asked him why. "I used to sleep raw, but I have to wear something now that Sarah's here. Except that I never wear the tops." He looked down at the soft thrust of her breasts, swollen and dark tipped in the aftermath of passion. He bent slowly and brushed his lips over them, tautening as the tips went hard involuntarily. "I've never felt more like a man than I feel when I touch you," he said roughly, his eyes closing, his brows knitting in the most exquisite pleasure.

She held his dark head against her, loving the feel of his warm mouth. "Are we going to sleep together?" she asked.

"We have to," he murmured, sliding his lips slowly over her breast. "I can't let you go."

She slid her arms around his neck as he lifted his head. "But, Sarah..."

"Sarah will be the first to find out we're going to be married," he murmured. "I'll get the license. We can have a blood test on Monday morning and the service two days later. Will that give you enough time to close out your apartment in San Antonio and change your mailing address?"

"Yes." She was breathless with his impatience, but not irritated. She wanted to live with him, and the sooner the better, before he woke up to what he was doing and changed his mind. She couldn't bear it if he'd only proposed in the heat of the moment.

He read that fear in her eyes. "I'm not going to change my mind. I'm not going to back out at the last minute or decide that I've satisfied my hunger for you and I don't need you anymore. I want you, Meredith," he emphasized. "I want to live with you, and not in some modern way with no ties and no legal status. To me, living with someone involves a thing called honor. It's a lost word in this society, but it still means a hell of a lot to me. I care enough to give you my name."

"I'll try to be a good wife," she said solemnly. "You won't mind if I just sit and stare at you sometimes, will you?"

He searched her eyes quietly. "Do you love me?"

Her lips trembled and she averted her gaze, focusing on his bare chest.

"All right. I won't force it out of you." He brought her forehead to his lips, his chest swelling with the knowledge that she did love him, even if she wouldn't admit it. He could see it in her eyes, feel it in her body. Apparently love could survive the cruelest blows, because God knows he'd hurt her enough to kill anything less. He closed his eyes and nuzzled his cheek against her soft dark hair. "I'll take care of you all my life," he promised. "Don't be afraid."

She trembled a little, because she was. Afraid that he didn't care enough, that he might regret his decision. He might fall in love again someday with someone else like Nina, and what would she do? She'd have to let him go....

It was happening so fast. Almost too fast. She hesitated. "Blake, maybe we should just get engaged . . ." she began worriedly.

He lifted his head and searched her eyes. "No."

"But—"

He put a long finger over her lips. "Do you remember what we said to each other when we came in here? About precautions?"

She colored. "Yes."

"Marriage and children are synonymous to me," he said quietly. "I think they are to you, too. I'm illegitimate, Meredith. I won't let my child be called what I was."

She sighed. "Does it really bother you so much?"

"I'd like to know who my father was at least," he replied. "Half my heritage is lost forever, because I have no idea who he was or what his background is. I can't tell Sarah anything about him. She'll ask someday."

"She'll understand, too," she replied. "She's a very special little girl. She's so much like you."

His green eyes searched hers. "We could have another daughter," he said. "Or a son."

She held her breath while he touched her flat stomach under the long open pajama top. Her heart went crazy when he looked down, watching the tips of her bare breasts harden helplessly.

She tried to pull the fabric together, but he caught her hands and held them gently.

"No," he said. "You can't imagine the pleasure it gives me just to see you like that."

Her breath sighed past her parted lips. "It's hard."

"I know." He lifted his eyes back to hers, searching them in a long, static silence. "It was for me, too, believe it or not. But I let you look at me, and I wasn't embarrassed." He smiled faintly. "I couldn't let Nina."

She reached up and touched her lips to his. "I'm glad," she said huskily.

He pulled her against him, nudging the pajama top out of the way so that her breasts brushed slowly against his hair-roughened chest, and she caught her breath with pleasure at the exquisite friction.

"We've got a lot to learn about this," he said softly. "We can learn it together."

"Yes." She touched her mouth to his throat, his collarbone. He took her head and guided her lips to his own nipples, groaning at the pleasure that shot through him when he felt the moist suction of her mouth.

"God, that feels good!" he ground out, forcing her mouth closer.

"Let's take our clothes off and experiment some more," she suggested brazenly, teasing him for the first time.

It delighted him. "You hussy!" he accused, and tugged her head up. His eyes were playful, and his face had never looked less hard.

"You started it," she pointed out, smiling back.

"But I can't finish it," he said ruefully. He sighed over her breasts before he buttoned them out of sight. "It's too soon," he said, answering the question in her eyes. "I don't want to rush you. You're much too new to this for any more experimenting."

She studied his face quietly. "How do you know?"

"Simple logic." He touched her lips. "And a book I read," he confessed, brushing his mouth over them. "In case I ever got this far with you, I wanted to make sure I knew enough so that I wouldn't make you afraid of me again."

"Oh, Blake." She hugged him hard, nestling her face against him. "Blake, I adore you."

His heart skipped when she said it. He smiled, aglow with satiation and the knowledge that she cared. "Lie down with me. We'll sleep in each others' arms."

She tingled all over as he pulled back the cover and tucked her in, turning out the light before he climbed in beside her. He drew her to him with a long, warm sigh and kissed her.

"Good night, little one," he whispered.

"Good night, Blake."

He closed his eyes, sure that he'd never been happier in his entire life. He pulled her closer and sighed when he felt her arms go around him. For a beginning, it was perfect.

But the next morning, when he awoke and found Meredith lying asleep in his bed, the perfection waned. His body surged at the sight of her, and he realized belatedly that the hunger he'd thought assuaged last night had only grown with feeding. He wanted her more now than ever, with a fever that actually made him shake as he looked at her sleeping body.

The realization terrified him. He'd never been vulnerable. Even Nina hadn't really knocked him off balance very far, or tested his control over his emotions. But Meredith did. She was the very air he breathed, the sun in his sky. He felt a rush of possessiveness when he looked at her, a desperate need to keep her, to protect her. He got out of bed and stared at her as if he'd gone mad. He'd sworn that he would never let her get to his heart, but last night he'd given her a lien on it. This morning, she owned him lock, stock and barrel.

He swallowed down a wave of nausea. The tender loving of the night faded into cold fear with the dawn. He didn't trust women, and now that distrust had extended itself to Meredith all over again. As long as he could persuade himself that it was only physical, marriage hadn't bothered him. But what he was feeling this morning gave new meaning to the situation. He could care for her. He could go crazy over her after a few more nights like last night. He could be so enamored of her that he'd do anything she wanted just to feel her arms around him. And that realization was what caught him by the throat—that he might not be able to keep his pride, his independence. He was afraid of her because he might love her, and he couldn't trust her enough to give in to her. She might be just like Nina. How could he know before it was too late?

Like a trapped animal, he felt the need to run, to get away, to think it through.

He got up and got dressed, taking one long, hungry look at Meredith before he forced himself to jerk open the door and go out. Last night everything had been so simple, until he'd touched her for the first time. And now he was mired up to his neck in quicksand. He didn't know what to do. He had the most ridiculous urge to go out and get Meredith an armload of roses. God knows, it must be the first stages of insanity, he thought as he went down the stairs and out the back door.

Nine

Meredith woke up slowly, aware of new surroundings and light coming into her room from the wrong direction. Then she moved, and her body told her that the light wasn't the only difference.

She sat up. She was in Blake's bedroom, in Blake's bed, wearing Blake's pajama top. Her face burned. The night before came back with startling clarity. She'd given in. More than given in. She'd participated wildly in what she and Blake had done together.

Her breath came unsteadily as wave after wave of remembered pleasure tingled in her sore body. She looked around, wondering if Blake was in the bathroom. But she spotted his pajama bottoms laid across the foot of the bed, and his boots were missing. They'd been sitting beside the armchair last night.

She got out of bed slowly, a little disoriented. "Bess!" she exclaimed, then remembered that she'd called Bess just after they'd gotten home last night to tell her that she was spending the night to help Blake with Sarah. Wouldn't Bess be grinning when she got back home this morning, she moaned to herself.

She put back on the clothes she'd taken off—the clothes that Blake had taken off for her, she corrected—and pulled on her socks and sneakers before she combed her hair.

In the mirror she could see the imprint of her head and Blake's on the pillows, and she blushed. Well, it was too late now for regrets. He'd said that they were getting married, so she might as well reconcile herself to her new status in his life. At least they were physically compatible and she loved him desperately. Perhaps someday he might learn to love her back. He was already different, mostly due, she was sure, to Sarah's gentle influence.

She opened the door and went to Sarah's room, but the little girl was nowhere in sight.

"If you're awake, breakfast is ready," Blake called from the foot of the staircase.

She looked down, thrilling to the sight of him, tall and dark headed, dressed in gray slacks and shirt with a light-weight tan sport coat and brown striped tie. He looked very elegant, and just a little somber.

That didn't bode well. She almost missed a step on her way down, nervous and shy with him after the night before. Her face was wildly colored and she couldn't look at him.

She paused two steps above him because his hand shot out and kept her there. His green eyes forced her to look at him, and he searched her face quietly.

"Come here," he said gently. "I've got something for you."

His big, lean hand curved possessively over hers and his fingers tangled in her cold ones as he led her into the hall and stopped her at the chair, which was covered with waxed paper that held dozens of small pink roses, their fragrance like perfume.

"For me?" she whispered, breathless.

"For you. I went out into the field and cut them early this morning."

She lifted them, burying her nose in their beautiful scent. "Oh, Blake," she moaned with pleasure, and looked up with her heart in her eyes.

He was glad then that he'd followed the crazy impulse in spite of his disturbing thoughts after waking. He bent and brushed his mouth over her forehead, his mood light. "I hoped you might like them," he murmured. "They looked as virginal as you did last night."

Her face felt like fire. "I'm not anymore," she said hesitantly.

He smiled slowly. "I'll carry last night in my heart until I die, Meredith Anne," he told her huskily. "It was everything it should have been. Magic."

She smiled into her roses, feeling all womanly and soft when he said things like that.

"Are you sorry that I took the choice away from you?" he asked unexpectedly, and his eyes were serious. "I carried you into my room without asking if it was what you wanted, and I didn't give you much chance to get away."

"Don't you think I could have gotten away if I'd really wanted to?" she asked honestly.

He smiled back at her. "No."

She traced rose petals. "Well, I could have. You didn't force me."

"In a way I did," he replied worriedly. "I didn't try to protect you. I don't want to force you into marriage with the threat of pregnancy."

Her eyebrows lifted. "Threat?" she picked up on the word. "Oh, no, it isn't that. A baby is..." Her breath caught as she searched his eyes and felt the hunger for a child. "Blake, a baby would be the sweetest thing in the world."

His heart began to race as he looked at her. "That's what I thought, too," he said. "That's why I didn't try to hold back." He smiled ruefully. "And the fact is, I don't think I could have. Years of abstinence makes it pretty hard for a man to keep his head."

Her eyes widened. "You meant it?" she exclaimed. "It was actually that long?"

He nodded. "Now I'm glad," he confessed. "It made it that much more intense with you." He framed her face with his lean hands and bent to savor her lips with his warm, moist ones. "So intense," he whispered roughly, "that I want it again and again and again. Every time I look at you, my body burns."

His mouth became demanding, and she felt the quick, violent response of his body to the feel of hers.

"So does mine," she whispered back, reaching up with her free hand to cling to his neck. "Blake," she moaned as his hands dropped to her hips and pulled her hard against him.

"God!" he groaned, and his mouth covered hers urgently.

Somewhere in the fever they were sharing, a door opened.

"Daddy? Meredith? Where are you?"

They broke apart with heated faces, trembling bodies and faintly crushed roses. "We're here," Blake said, recovering quickly. "We'll be there in a minute, Sarah. I was just giving Meredith her roses."

"Okay, Daddy. Aren't they nice, Merry?"

"Yes, darling," she murmured absently, but her eyes were on Blake as the child went back through to the kitchen.

"You aren't going home tonight," he said huskily. "I've got you and I'm keeping you, and to hell with gossip. I'll get the license tomorrow and arrange for blood tests with my doctor. I'll phone you from my office in the morning with the time. Meanwhile—" he smiled slowly "—you can go over to Bess's and get a change of clothes."

"What will I tell her?" she groaned.

"That we're getting married and you're taking care of Sarah while Mrs. Jackson's away," he said simply. He pulled her hand to his lips and kissed it warmly. "Sarah and I will even go with you to make things respectable. But first we'll have breakfast. Okay?"

She sighed with pure delight. "Okay. But I'll have to go to my apartment in San Antonio this week," she added.

"I'll take time off to go with you Tuesday. Sarah can come, too." He bent, half lifting her against his lean, hard body. "I'm not letting you out of my sight any more than I have to. You might decide to run for it."

"If you think that, you underestimate yourself," she murmured, and buried her face in his throat. "I don't have the strength to get away."

His hands contracted. "How sore are you?" he asked intimately.

She burrowed closer. "Blake...!"

"Is it bad?"

She grimaced and looked up at him, hesitating.

"Tell me the truth," he said. "It will spare us a lot of frustration later—if I start making love to you and have to stop."

"It's uncomfortable," she confessed finally, averting her eyes.

But he tilted her chin and forced her to look at him. "No secrets between us," he said. "Not ever. I want the truth, no matter how much it hurts, and you'll always get it from me."

"All right," she said. "I want it that way, too."

His eyes brushed over her soft features with lazy warmth. "You look very pretty without makeup," he remarked. "As pretty as these roses." He glanced at them and frowned. "We've bruised them a bit."

"They'll forgive us," she said. She reached up to kiss him softly. "Will your board of directors understand your taking two days off in one week?" she asked. "For a blood test and a license and then to go with me to Texas?"

"I haven't taken two days off in five years, so they'd better." He let her go. "Let's get breakfast. Then we'll go see Bess and Bobby."

She curled under his arm and, carrying her precious roses, let him guide her to the table.

It was cozy in the kitchen. Blake kept watching her and Meredith could hardly keep from bursting into song with the sheer joy of having him look at her that way. He might not love her, but he was already very, very possessive. And in time, love might come.

"Meredith and I are going to get married, Sarah," Blake said. "She's going to live with us and take care of you and write books."

Sarah's eyes lit up and the expression on the small face was humbling. "Are you, Merry? Are you going to be my mommy?" she asked, as if they were offering her the earth.

"Yes." Meredith smiled. "I'm going to be your mommy and hug and kiss you and tell you stories and—oh!"

Sarah ran to her like a whirlwind, almost knocking the breath out of her as she climbed onto her lap and clung, crying and mumbling things that Meredith couldn't understand.

"What is it, honey?" Blake asked, torn out of his normal calm by the child's totally unexpected reaction. He touched Sarah's dark hair gently. "What is it?" he repeated.

"I can stay now, can't I, Daddy?" Sarah asked him with wet red eyes. "I don't have to go. Merry is going to live with us and I'll be her little girl, too."

"Of course you can stay," Blake said shortly. "There was never any question of that."

"When I first came," she reminded him, "you said I could go to a . . . a home!"

"Damn my vicious tongue," Blake burst out. He got up, lifting Sarah out of Meredith's arms and into his own. He held her close, his green eyes steady on hers. "You'll never live in any home but mine," he said huskily. "You're my own flesh and blood, my own little girl. I . . ." He choked on the words. His jaw worked. "I . . . care for you—very much," he bit off finally.

Even at her age, Sarah seemed to realize what a difficult thing it was for him to say. She lowered her cheek to his shoulder with a sigh and smiled through her tears. "I love you, too, Daddy," she said.

Blake didn't know how he managed not to break down and cry. His arms contracted around her and he turned so that Meredith couldn't see his face. In all his life he'd never been so shaken.

"How about some more coffee?" Meredith asked gently. "I'll get it, okay?" She went to the stove to pour coffee from the percolator into the carafe, and her eyes were wet. She felt stunned by Blake's brief display of vulnerability, his hope for the future. If he could love Sarah, he could love others. She dabbed at her eyes and filled the carafe. Miracles did happen, after all.

When she turned back to the table, Sarah was sitting on Blake's lap. And she stayed there for the rest of breakfast, her small face full of love and wonder. Blake just looked smug.

"What about your work?" Blake asked when they'd finished breakfast and Sarah had excused herself to go and watch her eternal cartoons in the living room.

"I just need a place to set up my computer," she said.

His eyebrows arched. "What have you got?"

"An IBM compatible," she said. "Twin disk drives, over 600K memory, word processing software, a big daisy wheel printer and a modem."

"Come and look over my setup."

She let him take her hand and lead her into the study. "It's just like mine!" she exclaimed when she saw what he had on his desk.

He smiled at her. "A good omen?"

"Wonderful! Now we'll both have a spare," she said with a dancing glance.

"You can work here when I'm not home. And if you want to set up your equipment in the corner, we'll order another desk and some filing cabinets."

"It won't bother you?" she asked hesitantly. "I work odd hours. Sometimes, if I get on a streak, I may work into the small hours of the morning."

"I'm marrying you," he said. "That includes your job, your eccentricities, your bad habits and your temper. I don't mind what you do. You're entitled to a life that allows you the right to be your own person, to make your own dreams come true in business."

"I thought you were a chauvinist," she said. "That's the wrong attitude. You're supposed to refuse to let me work outside the home and say that no job is going to come before you."

He arched an eyebrow. "Okay, if that's what you want."

She hit his chest playfully. "Never mind. I like you better this way." She reached up and slid her arms around his neck. "Sarah says she won't mind if I hug and kiss her. So can I hug and kiss you, too?" she asked daringly.

His mouth quirked a little. "I guess so."

"You might show more enthusiasm," she said.

He bent his head and whispered, "I can't. You're sore."

She blushed and opened her mouth to protest just as his came down and settled over her lips. He kissed her gently, swinging her lightly in his arms from side to side as he held her mouth under his.

"That was nice," she told him huskily.

"I thought so, too." he let her go abruptly, the hardness back in his face. "I'll line up a charter flight to San Antonio for Tuesday. We can have your furniture sent out."

"It's a furnished apartment." She smiled. "All I have is my clothes, a few manuscripts and my computer stuff."

"Okay. We'll have that sent out."

"Blake, you're sure, aren't you?" she asked seriously.

"As sure as you are," he replied. "Now stop brooding over it. I'll get the license and set up the blood test for you tomorrow. Sarah can go with you to the doctor, because it will only take a minute."

"All right. It sounds like a nice day." She sighed.

"Every day is nice with you, Meredith," he said unexpectedly and with a wry smile.

But just as they started to go down to Bess's, a friend of Blake's arrived out of the blue, and Meredith went by herself, letting Sarah stay with her dad and his friend while she told Bess what was going on.

Bess was overwhelmed when she heard the news. "Congratulations!" She laughed. "It's the best thing that could have happened to both of you. You'll make a good marriage."

"Oh, I hope so." Meredith sighed. "I'll do my best, and at least Blake likes me."

"At least," Bess said, and laughed. "If you need witnesses, Bobby and I will be glad to volunteer. Elissa and King, too."

"You can all come," Meredith promised. "I'll need as much moral support as I can get." She shook her head. "It seems like a beautiful dream. I hope I don't wake up. Well, I'd better get my things and get back up to his place. I hope you don't mind, but he, uh, doesn't want me out of his sight until the ceremony Wednesday."

"Fast mover, isn't he?" Bess grinned and hugged her friend warmly. "I'm so happy for you, Merry. And for Blake and Sarah. You'll make a lovely family."

Meredith thought so, too. She carried her single suitcase out to the Porsche and drove up in front of Blake's house. Sarah Jane met her at the door as she set her case down, and Blake came out of the living room smiling.

"Well, what did she say?" he asked. He answered her silent glance into the living room. "He's gone. What did Bess say?"

"She said congratulations." Meredith laughed. "And that we'll make a lovely family."

"Indeed we will," Blake murmured gently.

"Merry, can I be a flower girl?" Sarah asked from behind her.

"You certainly can," Meredith promised, kneeling beside the child to hug her. "You can carry an armload of roses."

"But, Merry, they're all crushed."

"Daddy will cut some more," Meredith said, warming when she remembered how the roses had gotten crushed. She glanced at Blake and the look in his eyes made her blush.

The next two days went by in an unreal rush. The blood tests were done, the license obtained, and a minister was lined up to perform the ceremony at the local Baptist church where Meredith's parents had worshipped when she was a child. For reasons that Meredith still didn't understand, Blake had given her a guest room to sleep in until the wedding, and although he'd been friendly enough, he hadn't really attempted to make love to her. She preferred to think it was because she was still uncomfortable from their first time rather than because he had any regrets.

The ceremony was held late Wednesday afternoon, with King and Elissa Roper and Bess and Bobby for witnesses. Meredith said her vows with tears in her eyes, so happy that her heart felt like it would overflow.

She'd bought a white linen suit to be married in, with a tiny pillbox hat covered in lace. It was so sweet when Blake put the ring on her finger and lifted the veil to kiss her. She felt like Sleeping Beauty, as if she'd been asleep for years and years and now was waking to the most wonderful reality.

The reception was held at the Ropers' sprawling white frame house outside Jack's Corner, and Danielle and Sarah Jane played quietly while the adults enjoyed champagne punch and a lavish catered buffet.

"You didn't have to go to this kind of expense, for God's sake," Blake muttered to big King Roper.

King pursed his lips and his dark eyes sparkled. "Yes, I did. Having you get close enough to a woman to marry again deserved something spectacular." He glanced at Meredith, who was talking animatedly to Elissa and Bess a few feet away while Bobby, the exact opposite in coloring to his half-brother, King, was watching the kids play.

"She's a dish," King remarked. "And we all know how she felt about you when she left here." His dark eyes caught Blake's green ones. "It's not a good thing to live alone. A wife and children make all the difference. I know mine do."

"Sarah likes her," Blake replied, sipping punch as his eyes slid over Meredith's exquisite figure like a paintbrush. "She's a born mother."

King smiled. "Thinking of a large family, are you?"

Blake glared at him. "I've only just got married."

"Speaking of which, why aren't you two going on a honeymoon?"

"I'd like that," Blake confessed. "But neither Meredith nor I like the idea of leaving Sarah behind while we have one. She's had enough insecurity for one month. Anyway," he added, "Meredith's got that autographing in town Saturday, and she doesn't want to disappoint the bookstore."

"She always was a sweet woman," King remarked. "I remember her ragged and barefoot as a child, helping her mother carry eggs to sell at Mackelroy's Grocery. She never minded hard work. In that," he added with a glance at his friend, "she's a lot like you."

Blake smiled faintly. "I didn't have a choice. It was work or starve in my case. Now that I'm in the habit, I can't quit."

King eyed him solemnly. "Don't ever let work come before Meredith and Sarah," he cautioned. "Bobby had to find that out the hard way, and he barely realized it in time."

Blake was looking at Meredith with faint hunger in his narrow eyes. "It would take more than a job to overshadow Meredith," he said without thinking. He finished his punch. "And we'd better get going. I've got reservations at the Sun Room for six o'clock. You're sure you and Elissa don't mind having Sarah for the night?"

"Not at all. And she loves the idea of sleeping in Danielle's room," King assured him. "If she needs you, I promise we'll call, even if it's two in the morning. Fair enough?" he added when he saw the worry in Blake's eyes.

"Fair enough," Blake said with a sigh.

A few minutes later, Blake and Meredith said their goodbyes, kissed Sarah good-night and went to the Sun Room for an expensive wedding supper.

"I still can't quite believe it," Meredith confessed with a smile as she looked at her husband across the table. "That we're married," she added.

"I know what you mean," he said quietly. His eyes caressed her face. "I swore when Nina left that I'd never marry again. But it seemed the most natural thing in the world with you."

She smiled. "I hope I don't disappoint you. I can cook and clean, but I'm not terribly domestic, and when I'm writing, sometimes I pour coffee over ice and put mashed potatoes in the icebox and make coffee without putting a filter in it. I'm sort of absentminded."

"As long as you remember me once in a while, I won't complain," he promised. "Eat your dessert before it melts."

She picked up a spoon to start on her baked alaska. "Sarah was so happy." She sighed.

"You'll be good for her." He sipped his coffee and watched Meredith closely. "You'll be good for both of us."

Meredith felt as if she were riding on a cloud for the rest of the evening. The Sun Room had a dance band as well as a wonderful restaurant. They danced until late, and Meredith was concealing a yawn when they got home.

"Thank you for my honeymoon," she said with a mischievous smile when they were standing together in the hall. "It was wonderful."

"Later on I'll give you a proper one," he promised. "We'll go away for several days. To Europe or the Caribbean."

"Let's go to Australia and stay on a cattle station," she suggested. "I wrote about one of those in my last book, and it sounded like a great place to visit."

"Haven't you traveled?" he asked.

"Just to the Bahamas and Mexico," she said. "It was great, but no place is really exciting when you have to see it alone."

"I know what you mean." He pulled her against him and bent to kiss her. "You still taste of ice cream," he murmured, and kissed her again.

"You taste of coffee." She linked her arms around his neck and smiled at him. "I want to ask you something."

"Be my guest."

"Do you have any deeply buried scruples about intimacy after marriage?" she asked somberly. "I mean, I wouldn't want to cause you any trauma."

He smiled in spite of himself. "No," he replied. "I don't think I have any buried scruples about it. Why? Were you thinking of seducing me?"

"I would if I knew how," she assured him. She smiled impishly. "Could you give me a few pointers?"

He reached down and picked her up in his arms. "I think I might be able to help you out," he said. He started for the staircase with his lips brushing hers. "It might take a while," he added under his breath. "You don't mind, do you? You don't have any pressing appointments in the next few hours...?"

"Only one. With you," she whispered, and pressed her open mouth hungrily to his, shivering with delight as his tongue pushed softly inside it and tasted her. She moaned with the aching pleasure.

His lips drew back a little. "I like that," he whispered huskily. "Make a lot of noise. Tonight there's no one to hear you except me."

Her teeth tugged at his lower lip and she obliged him with a slow, sultry moan that caused his mouth to grow rough with desire. She smiled under the heat of the kiss, and when he lifted his head and saw her expression, for just an instant he wondered if, like Nina, she was pretending pleasure that she didn't feel. And then he saw her eyes. And all his doubts fell away as his mouth bit hungrily into hers. He thought that in all his life he'd never seen such a fierce passion in a woman's soft eyes....

This time he left the lights on. He undressed her slowly, drawing it out, making her dizzy with pleasure as he kissed every inch of her as he uncovered her body. When the clothes were off, his mouth smoothed over her adoringly, lingering on her soft, warm breasts. He'd never realized how infallible instinct was until now. Apparently it didn't matter how skilled he was. She cared for him, and that made her delightfully receptive to anything he wanted. His heart swelled with the knowledge.

By the time he'd undressed, she was trembling, her body waiting, her eyes so full of warm adoration that he felt like a lonely traveler finally coming home. This was nothing like the indifference Nina had shown when he'd touched her. He looked at Meredith's lovely face and wanted nothing more in life than her arms around him.

She raised her feverish eyes to his, drowning in their green glitter. His lips parted and she trembled, because he wasn't in any hurry.

His hard mouth brushed at hers while his hands touched her with reverence. His wife. Meredith was his wife, and she wanted him. He groaned softly. "Merry, love me," he whispered as his mouth bit hungrily into hers. "Love me."

She felt her body trembling with delight as she heard the soft words and wondered dizzily if he even realized what he was saying. Poor, lonely man. . . .

Her arms went around him hungrily and she kissed him back, willing to give him anything as tenderness and love welled up within her.

"You're . . . killing me," she bit off minutes later, when his slow, exquisitely tender caresses were making her shudder with need for him.

"Liar," he told her, smiling gently at her even through his own trembling need. He moved suddenly, and watched her eyes dilate, felt her body react. "That's it. Help me," he coaxed. "Show me what you want, little one. Let me . . . love you," he groaned when she lifted her body up into his.

Blinded with the passion they were sharing, she pulled his head down to her mouth and kissed him with all the lonely years and all her smothered love in her lips. She felt his powerful body tremble until it gave way under his hunger for her and he overwhelmed her with exquisite tenderness.

Her cry was echoed in his as unbearable pleasure bound them, lifted them together in a fierce buffeting embrace, and they clung to each other as the wave of fulfillment hit them together.

Meredith could barely breathe when she felt the full weight of Blake's body against her. He was shivering, and her arms contracted around him.

"Darling," she whispered. Her lips touched his cheek, his mouth, his throat, damp with sweat. "Darling, darling...!"

The endearment went through his weary body like an electric current. He returned her tender kisses, smoothing her bare body against his and loving the soft curves caressing him. His hands felt almost too rough to be touching her. He savored the warm silk of her skin, the cologne scent of her, the pleasure of just being close to her.

Somewhere in the back of his mind, he remembered whispering to her to love him. He buried his mouth in her throat, kissing it hungrily as his need broke through his reserve and made him just temporarily vulnerable.

He pulled her into the hair-roughened curve of his chest and thighs, holding her with a new kind of possessiveness. His mouth brushed her forehead and her closed eyes with breathless tenderness. He felt the tension of pleasure slowly relax in her soft body, as it had in his own.

"I've been alone all my life until now," he said quietly, his face solemn. "I never realized how cold it was until you warmed me."

Tears formed in her eyes. "I'll warm you all my life if you'll let me," she assured him huskily.

He searched her soft face and bent to take her mouth under his. "Warm me now," he breathed against her lips, and his hands slid to her hips. As he pulled her close, he heard her voice, heard the soft endearment that broke from her lips, and his heart almost burst with delight that she cared too much to be capable of hiding it.

Later, curled up together with the lights out, Blake lay

awake long after Meredith was enveloped in contented sleep. He couldn't quite believe what had happened so quickly in his life. He'd been alone, and now he had a daughter and a loving wife, and the way it was affecting him made him nervous.

Something had happened tonight with Meredith. Something incredible. It hadn't been just the satisfying of a physical desire anymore. It went much deeper than that. There was something reverent about the way they made love, about the tenderness they gave to each other. He was being taken over by Meredith and he had cold feet. Could he really trust her not to walk out on him as Nina had? If he let himself fall in love with her, would she betray him? He looked down at her sleeping face, and even in the darkness he could see its warm glow. The distrust relaxed out of him. He could trust her.

Of course he could, he told himself firmly. After all, he could live with her profession and she'd have Sarah to keep her busy. Her writing wasn't going to interfere in their lives. He'd make sure of it.

Ten

But Meredith's job did interfere with their marriage. Her autographing session was the first indication of it. Blake and Sarah had gone to the bookstore Saturday to watch, and Blake had been fascinated by the number of people who'd come to have her sign their books. Dressed in a very sexy green-and-white ensemble, with a big white hat to match, Meredith looked very much the successful, urbane author. And she was suddenly speaking a language he didn't understand. Her instant rapport with people fascinated and disturbed him. He didn't get along well with people, and he certainly didn't seek them out. If she was really as gregarious as she seemed and started to expect to throw lavish parties and have weekend guests, things were going to get sticky pretty fast.

As it happened, she wasn't a party girl. But she did have to do a lot of traveling in connection with the release of her latest book.

Blake went through the ceiling when she announced her third out-of-state trip in less than three weeks.

"I won't have it," he said coldly, bracing her in the study.

"*You* won't have it?" Meredith replied with equal hauteur. "You told me when we married that you didn't mind if I worked."

"And I don't, but this isn't working. It's jet-setting," he argued. "My God, you're never here! Amie's spending most of her time baby-sitting Sarah because you're forever getting on some damned airplane!"

"I know," Meredith said miserably. "And I'm sorry. But I made this commitment to promote the book before I married you. You of all people wouldn't want me to go back on my word."

"Wouldn't I?" he demanded, and he looked like the old Blake, all bristling masculinity and outraged pride. "Stay home, Meredith."

"Or what?" she challenged, refusing to be ordered about like a child of Sarah's age. "What did you have in mind, tying me to a tree out in the backyard? Or moving to your club in town? You can't, you know, you don't have a club in town."

"I could use one," he muttered darkly. "Okay, honey. If you want the job that much, go do it. But until you come to grips with the fact that this is a marriage, not a limited social engagement, I'm sleeping in the guest room."

"Go ahead," she said recklessly. "I don't care. I won't be here!"

"Isn't that the gospel truth," he said, glaring at her.

She turned on her heel and went to pack.

From then on, everything went downhill between them. She felt an occasional twinge of guilt as Blake reverted to

his old, cold self. He was polite to her, but nothing more.
He didn't touch her or talk to her. He acted as if she were
a houseguest and treated her accordingly. It was a night-
marish change from the first days of their marriage, when
every night had been a new and exciting adventure, when
their closeness in bed had fostered an even deeper closeness the rest of the time. She'd been sure that he was
halfway in love with her. And then her traveling had
started to irritate him. Now he was like a stranger, and
Meredith tossed and turned in the big bed every night, all
alone. In the back of her mind, the knowledge that she had
failed to conceive ate away at her confidence. As the days
went on, Blake was becoming colder and colder.

Only with Sarah was he different. That was amusing,
and Meredith laughed at the spectacle of Blake being followed relentlessly every step he took by Sarah Jane. She
was right behind him all weekend, watching him talk to the
men, sitting with him while he did the books, riding with
him when he went out over the fields in the pickup truck
to see about fences and cattle and feed. Sarah Jane was his
shadow, and he smiled tolerantly at her attempts to imi-
tate his long strides and his habit of ramming his hands in
his pockets and rocking back on his heels when he talked.
Sarah was sublimely happy. Meredith was sublimely miserable.

She tried once to talk to Blake, to make him understand that it wouldn't always be this way. But he walked
off even as she began.

"Put it in your memoirs, Mrs. Donavan," he said with
a mocking smile. "Your readers might find it interesting."

In other words, he didn't. Meredith choked back tears
and went to her computer to work on her next book. It was
taking much longer than she'd expected, and the tense

emotional climate in the house wasn't helping things along.
It was hard to feel romantic enough to write a love scene
when her own husband refused to touch her or spend five
minutes in a room with her when eating wasn't involved,
or watching the news on television.

"You're losing weight," Bess commented one day at
lunch when Meredith had escaped to her house to avoid the
cold silence at home.

"I'm not surprised." Meredith sighed. "It's an ordeal
to eat over there. Blake glares at me or ignores me, de-
pending on his mood. I tried to explain that it wasn't going
to be like this every time a book came out, but he refuses
to listen."

"Maybe he's afraid to listen," Bess said sagely. "Blake's
been alone a long time, and he doesn't really trust women.
Maybe he's trying to withdraw before he gets in over his
head. In which case—" she grinned "—it could be a good
omen. What if he's falling in love with you and trying to
fight it? Wouldn't he act just that way?"

"No normal man would," Meredith grumbled.

"Bobby did. So did King, according to Elissa. Men are
really strange creatures when their emotions get stirred
up." She cocked her blond head and stared at Meredith.
"You might put on your sexiest negligee and give him
hell."

"There's a thought. But he'd probably toss me out the
window if I dared."

"You underestimate yourself."

"All the same, it's his heart I want to reach. I can't really
do that in bed," Meredith said with sad eyes. "He's always wanted me. But I want more. I'm greedy. I want him
to love me."

"Give it time. He'll come around eventually."

"Meanwhile I'm miserable," Meredith said. "At least he and Sarah are getting along like a house on fire. They're inseparable."

"Camouflage," Bess said. "He's using her to keep you at bay."

"He wouldn't."

"You greenhorn." Bess sighed. "I wish I could make you listen."

"Me, too." Meredith got up. "I've got to go. I have to fly to Boston for a signing in the morning. And I haven't told Blake yet." She grimaced. "He's been in an explosive mood for two weeks. This will sure light the fuse, I'm afraid."

"Do you have to go?"

She nodded. "It's the very last trip, but I did promise, and the bookseller is a friend of mine. I can't let her down."

Bess searched Meredith's face. "Better Blake than her?" she asked quietly. "It seems to me, from an objective standpoint, that you're running as hard from this relationship as he is. Do you really have to make these trips, or are you doing it to spite him, to prove your independence?"

"I can't let him own me," Meredith said stubbornly.

"Good for you. But a man like that isn't going to be owned, either. You're going to have to compromise if you want to keep him."

Meredith felt herself going pale. "What do you mean, if I want to keep him?"

"Just that you could drive him away. He isn't like other men. He's been kicked around too much already. His pride won't take much more abuse. You see these trips as simple tours," she explained. "Blake sees that you prefer your work to him."

Meredith felt sick. "No. He couldn't think . . ."

"I did with Bobby," Bess said simply. "I was sure that he would walk over my dying body to get to the office. I very nearly left him because of it. I couldn't bear being second best." Her eyes narrowed. "Neither can Blake. So look out."

"I've been blind," Meredith groaned. She wrapped her arms around herself. "I thought it was important not to be led around like a dumb animal, so I was fighting for my independence." She closed her eyes. "I never dreamed he'd think I considered him less important than writing."

"If you want some expert advice, tell him while there's still time," Bess suggested.

Meredith hugged the blond-haired woman. "Thanks," she said huskily. "I love him so much, you know, and it was like a dream come true when he married me. Maybe I was afraid to let myself be happy with him, afraid of being hurt, of losing him again. I guess I just lost my perspective."

"Blake probably lost his for the same reason. Get over there and fight for what you have."

"Ever thought about joining the army?" Meredith murmured on her way out the door. "You'd make a dandy drill sergeant."

"The marines offered, but then I found out they expected me to take showers with the men." Bess grinned. "Bobby would never approve of that!"

Meredith laughed and waved as she got into her car and sped back up to the house. Bless Bess for making things so clear. It was going to be all right now. She'd tell Blake the real reason she'd insisted on the tours, and it would smooth over the tension.

She got out of the car and ran into the house, but there was no sound. Odd. She was sure Sarah had been playing in the living room.

She wandered into the kitchen, but there was no one there except Amie.

"Where is everybody?" Meredith asked, excitement shining in her eyes as she savored speaking to Blake.

Amie looked at her worriedly. "Surely Blake told you, Merry," she said hesitantly.

Meredith blinked. "Told me what?"

"Why, that he was taking Sarah to the Bahamas for a few days," Amie said, dropping the bombshell.

Meredith knew her face was like rice paper, but she managed to smile. "Oh. Yes. Of course. It slipped my mind."

"You're crying!" Amie put down her dishcloth and hugged Meredith. "Poor little thing," she mumbled, patting the weeping woman. "He didn't tell you, did he?"

"No."

"I'm sorry."

Meredith reached into her pocket for a tissue and wiped her red eyes. "I've given him a hard time lately," she said. "It's no more than I deserve." She took a deep breath. "I have to fly to Boston in the morning, but when I come back, that's the end of my traveling. I won't go on tour again. Not ever."

Amie searched her white face. "Don't do that," she said unexpectedly.

"What?"

"Don't do it. If you let him get the upper hand now, if you ever let him start ordering your life, you'll never be your own person again," she said simply. "He's a good man in many ways, but he has a domineering streak a mile wide. If you let him, he'll tell you how to breathe. I know you want peace with him, but don't sacrifice your freedom for it.''

Meredith felt torn. Bess had said give in, Amie was saying don't. She didn't know what to do anymore. Who was right? And what should she do?

Her heart shattered, she went upstairs to pack. What had begun as a beautiful marriage had turned sour. It was partly her fault, but Blake was as much to blame. She wondered if he was able to admit fault. Somehow she didn't think so.

Boston was lovely. She did her autographing and stayed an extra day to enjoy the historic places and spend a little time in the local library. But her heart was broken. Blake had gone away without her, without even asking if she wanted to go with him. She didn't know if she even wanted to go home again.

She did go home again, of course—to an empty house. She and Amie ate together and Meredith worked on her newest book because there was nothing else to do. And all the while she wondered what Blake and Sarah were doing. Most of all, she wondered if his eye was wandering to a more domestic kind of woman, one who would be content to stay at home and have his babies.

She stopped writing and sat with her head in her hands, daydreaming about having Blake's child. Even though they hadn't taken precautions she hadn't conceived. In a way that was a shame. A baby might have helped bring them together. On the other hand, if Blake decided to leave her, it would be better for both of them if there were no blood ties.

Leave her. She closed her eyes. *If Blake should leave her...* She couldn't bear even to think of it. She loved him so, missed him so. Tears ran down her cheeks, blinding her. If only he could love her back. . . .

Blake, meanwhile, was riding around New Providence in a jitney with Sarah at his side, smiling as she enthused over the beautiful flowers and the unbelievable colors of the ocean and the whiteness of the sand. If Meredith had been with them, it would truly have been paradise.

His eyes darkened at the thought. Meredith. He hadn't really given her a chance, he supposed. Her traveling made him mad and he'd pushed her out of his life because she refused to stop. In a way he was glad she had the spirit to stand up to him. But in another, he felt miserable because she was telling him he was nothing compared to her career. It hurt far more than Nina's betrayal. Because he hadn't loved Nina. And he...cared...for Meredith.

He couldn't bear to think about her. He'd come down here with Sarah to hurt her. Probably she was in tears when Amie told her they had gone. His face hardened. She was going to take a long time to forgive him for that slap in the face. He was sorry he'd done it. He'd been hurting and wanted to strike back, but now it all seemed so petty and unnecessary. Being cruel wasn't going to win Meredith back. He sighed. He didn't quite have the hang of marriage yet. But he was going to work at learning how when he got back. He had to. He couldn't bear to lose Meredith. These past few cold weeks had made his life hell, especially at night. He missed her soft body, her quiet breathing next to him. He missed her laughter and the lazy talks they'd had late at night. He missed a lot. He only hoped he hadn't left things too late.

"Sarah," he said, "how would you like to go home tomorrow?"

"I'd like that, Daddy," she said. "I miss Merry something awful!"

"Yes, so do I," he murmured under his breath.

Meredith was sitting at the computer with her reading glasses on when she heard the front door open.

"Merry!" Sarah Jane cried, and flung herself at Meredith to hug her convulsively. "Merry, why didn't you come with us? We had such fun, but it was lonely without you!"

"It was lonely without you, too, baby." Meredith sighed, hugging Sarah close.

She heard Blake's step in the hall, and her heart ran away. Her body quivered. She didn't look up because she didn't dare. He'd hurt her enough. She wasn't giving him any more openings.

"Hello, Meredith," he said quietly.

She lifted cool gray eyes to his. "Hello, Blake. I hope you had a pleasant time."

He shifted. He had a faint sunburn, but he looked almost gaunt. She realized that he'd honed down a little, too, during their cold war, and guilt made her throat constrict.

"It was all right," he said coolly. "How have you been?"

"Oh, I've had a ball," she said nervously, hiding her lack of confidence from him. She smiled at Sarah. "I went to autograph in Boston and researched a new book while I was there."

Blake's expression closed up. He'd imagined her sitting home crying, and she'd been in Boston working on another damned book. He turned on his heel without another word and left her sitting there.

"And I'm going to have a party and everything, Merry, 'cause Daddy said so!" Sarah was chattering excitedly. She looked pretty. Her hair was neatly combed and she had on a soft, lightweight cotton dress with red and beige patterns on it, obviously bought for her in the Bahamas. Blake had even put a bow in her hair.

"A party?" Meredith echoed. She hadn't been listening, because the cold look on Blake's face had hit her hard. She'd put her foot in it again by raving about her trip.

"My birthday, Merry!" Sarah said with forced patience.

"That's right," Meredith said. "It's coming up."

"And we have to have a party," Sarah said. "Dani can come, and you and Daddy, and we can have cake."

"And ice cream," Meredith said, smiling at the child's obvious excitement. "We might even have balloons and a clown. Would you like that?"

"Oh, yes!"

"When are we having the party?" Meredith asked.

"Next Saturday," Sarah said.

"Well, I'll see what I can do." She took off her reading glasses and Sarah picked them up and tried to look through them, making a face when everything was blurry.

Mrs. Jackson fixed the birthday cake with a favorite cartoon character of Sarah's on the top and Meredith arranged for a local clown to come to the party to entertain the children. She invited Dani and some of Dani's friends, anticipating bedlam. Maybe if they ate in the kitchen, it would be less messy.

"Why should they eat in the kitchen?" Blake asked icily when Meredith got up her nerve the day of the party to approach him about it. "They're children, not animals. They can eat in the dining room."

Meredith curtsied and smiled. "Yes, my lord," she said. "Anything you say, sir."

"That isn't funny," he said. He stalked out of the room and Meredith stuck out her tongue at him.

"Reverting to childhood?" Mrs. Jackson asked with a gleam in her eye as she opened the hutch to get out plates and glasses, since the party was less than two hours away.

"I guess so. He infuriates me!" She sighed. "He says we have to have it in here. Doesn't he know that cake and ice cream are terrible on carpet?"

"Not yet," Amie said with her tongue in her cheek. "But he will."

Meredith smiled conspiratorially at her. "Yes, he certainly will."

They had the party in the dining room. There were seven four-year-olds. In the middle of the cake and ice cream, they had a food fight. By the time Meredith and Elissa, who'd volunteered to help out, got them stopped, the room looked like a child's attempt at camouflage. There was ice cream on the carpet, the hutch, the tablecloth, and even tiny splatters on Blake's elegant crystal chandelier. Waterford crystal, too, Meredith mused as she studied the chocolate spots there. The chairs were smeared with vanilla cake and white frosting, and underfoot there was enough cake to feed several hungry mice.

"Isn't this fun, Merry?" Sarah Jane exclaimed with a chocolate ring around her mouth and frosting in her hair.

"Yes, darling," Meredith agreed wholeheartedly. "It's fun, indeed. I can hardly wait until your daddy gets here."

Just as she said that, Sarah Jane's daddy walked in the door and stopped as if he'd been hit in the knee with a bat. His lower lip fell a fraction of an inch and he stared at the table and children as if he'd never seen either before.

He lifted a finger and turned to Meredith to say something.

"Isn't it just such fun?" Meredith asked brightly. "We had a food fight. And then we had chocolate warfare. I'm afraid your chandelier became a casualty, but, then, you'll have *such* fun hosing it down. . . ."

Blake's face was getting redder by the instant. He glared at Meredith and went straight through to the kitchen.

Seconds later, Meredith could hear his deep, slow voice giving Amie hell on the half-shell, and then the back door slammed hard enough to shake the room.

Elissa's twinkling blue eyes met Meredith's gray ones. "My, my, and he insisted on the dining room? Where do you think he's gone?"

"To get a hose, I expect," Meredith commented, and then broke into laughter.

"I wouldn't laugh too loud," Elissa cautioned as she helped mop Dani's face.

The clown arrived just after the children were tidied, and he kept them occupied in the living room with Elissa while Meredith and Amie began the monumental task of cleaning the dining room.

Meredith was on the floor with a wet sponge and carpet cleaner when Blake came in, followed by two rugged looking men wearing uniforms. Without a word, he tugged Meredith up by the arm, took the sponge from her hand, tossed it to one of the men and guided her into the living room.

He left her there without a word. Belatedly she realized that he'd gone to get some cleaning men to take care of the mess. Oddly, it made her want to cry. His thoughtfulness had surprised her. Or maybe it was his conscience. Either way, she thought, it had been kind of him to do that for Amie and her.

Seconds later, Amie was pulled into the living room. She stared at Meredith and shrugged. Then she smiled and sat down to enjoy the clown with the children.

It was, Sarah Jane said after the guests had gone, the best party in the whole world.

"I made five new friends, Merry," she told Meredith gaily. "And they liked me!"

"Most everyone likes you, darling," Meredith said, kneeling to hug her. Her white-and-pink dress was liberally stained with chocolate and candy, but that's what parties were for, Meredith told herself. "Especially me," she added with a big kiss.

Sarah Jane hugged her tight. "I love you, Merry." She sighed. "I just wish . . ."

"Wish what, pet?"

"I wish my daddy loved you," she said, and her big green eyes looked sadly at Meredith.

Meredith hadn't realized until then how perceptive Sarah was. Her face lost its glow. She forced a smile. "It's hard to explain about grown-ups, Sarah," she said finally. "Your daddy and I have disagreed about some things, that's all."

"Why not tell her the truth?" Blake demanded coldly from the doorway. "Why not tell her that your writing comes before she does, and before I do, and that you just don't care enough to stay home?"

"That's not true!" Meredith got to her feet, her eyes flashing. "You won't even listen to my side of it, Blake!"

"Why bother?" He laughed mockingly. "Your side isn't worth hearing."

"And yours is?"

Neither of them noticed Sarah Jane's soft gasp, or the sudden paleness of her little face. Neither of them saw the tears gather in her green eyes and start to flow down her cheeks. Neither of them knew the traumatic effect the argument was having on her, bringing back memories of fights between her mother and stepfather and the violence that had highlighted most of her young life.

She sobbed silently and suddenly turned and slipped from the room, hurrying up the staircase.

"Your pride is going to destroy our marriage," Meredith raged at Blake. "You just can't stand the idea of letting me work, or giving me any freedom at all. You want me to stay home and look after Sarah and have babies—"

"Writers don't have babies," he said curtly. "It's too demeaning and limiting."

She felt her face go pale. "I never said that, Blake," she said. "I haven't done anything to prevent a baby." She lowered her eyes to the carpet and hoped the glitter of her tears wouldn't show. "I just can't...can't seem to get pregnant."

His breath sighed out roughly. He hadn't meant to say such a cruel thing. It was cruel, too, judging by the look on her face. She seemed to really want a child, and that warmed him.

He moved forward a little, his hand going out to touch her hair. "I didn't mean that," he said awkwardly.

She looked up. There were tears in her eyes. "Blake," she whispered achingly, and lifted her arms.

He cursed his own vulnerability even as he reached for her, lifting her hard against him, holding her close. "Don't cry, little one," he said against her ear as she sobbed out the frustration and loneliness and fear of the past few weeks against his broad shoulder.

"There's something...something *wrong* with me," she wailed.

"No, there isn't." He nuzzled his cheek against hers. "Unless you count a husband with an overdose of pride. You're right. It was just feeling second best, that's all. You can't stay home all the time."

"I promised I'd go on tour," she said huskily. "I didn't want to. But then, when I kept not getting pregnant, I hated having so much time to sit and worry about it." Her arms tightened around his neck. "I wanted to give you a son...."

His arms contracted. He'd never considered that as a reason for her wandering. He'd never dreamed she wanted a child so much.

"We've been married only a few weeks," he whispered at her ear. "And the past several, I've been sleeping in another room." He smiled faintly in spite of himself. "It takes a man and a woman to make babies. You can't do it by yourself."

She laughed softly, and he felt warm all over at the sound, because she hadn't laughed in a long time.

"If you want to get pregnant, Mrs. Donavan, you'll have to have a little help."

She drew in a breath and looked into his soft green eyes. "Could you do that for me?" she whispered playfully. "I mean, I know it would be a sacrifice and all, but I'd be *sooo* grateful."

He laughed, too. The joy came back into his life again. She was beautiful, he thought, studying her face. And he cared so damned much. His eyes darkened and the smile faded. Cared. No. It was more. Far more than that. He...loved.

"Kiss me," he said, bending to her soft mouth. "It's been so long, honey. So long!"

His mouth covered hers hungrily, and she felt her body melting into him, aching for his touch, for the crush of his mouth on her soft lips. She moaned, and his kiss became suddenly ardent and demanding.

"Merry?" Mrs. Jackson called suddenly from the hall.

Blake and Meredith broke apart with breathless reluctance, but there was a strange note in Amie's usually calm voice.

Meredith moved to the closed door and opened it. "Amie, what is it?" she asked, wondering at the closed door, because it had been open when Sarah was in the room with them—"Where's Sarah!" Meredith asked suddenly.

Blake felt himself pale when he remembered the argument. Sarah Jane had heard.

Amie grimaced. "I don't know where she is. I can't find her," she said. "She isn't in her room. And it's raining outside."

It was thundering, too. And it was almost dark. Meredith and Blake didn't waste time on words. They rushed down the hall and out the back door, forgoing rain gear in their haste to find the child they'd unknowingly sent running out into the stormy night.

Eleven

Blake wanted to throw things. He searched the stable, every nook and cranny of it, and every one of the outbuildings, with Meredith quiet and worried beside him. The rain was coming down heavier now, and the last bit of light had left the sky, except for the occasional lightning.

"Where can she be?" Meredith groaned as they stood in the doorway of the barn and looked out into the night.

"I don't know," Blake said heavily. "God, I could kick myself!"

She slid her hand into his big one and held on tight. "I'm every bit as responsible as you are, Blake," she said gently. "I was being stubborn and proud, too." She went close to him, nuzzling her cheek against his broad chest. "I'm sorry for all of it. I never looked at things from your point of view."

"That goes double for me." He bent and kissed her forehead. "I wish we'd remembered that Sarah was in the room. She's had nightmares about arguments her mother and stepfather used to have. Violence upsets her. Any kind of violence. When I yelled at her about getting in the corral with the horse she—" He stopped dead, remembering. He straightened. "No," he said to himself. "No, she couldn't be. That would be too easy, wouldn't it?"

"What would?" Meredith asked as she tried to follow his train of thought.

"Come on!"

He ran toward the house, tugging her along behind him. They were both soaked. Meredith's blouse was plastered to her skin, and her hair hung in wet tangles over her face. Blake didn't look much better. His tan shirt was so wet that she could see right through it to the thick tangle of black hair on his chest.

"Did you find her?" Amie asked worriedly from the sink, where she was washing dishes.

"I'm almost sure I have," Blake said. He dragged Meredith with him and shot up the staircase.

He opened the door to Sarah's room, went straight to the closet and, with a silent prayer, opened it.

And there was Sarah Jane, sobbing silently in the very far corner of the closet floor, under all her pretty things.

"You . . . hate each other," Sarah sobbed, "just like my mommy and Daddy Brad. I'll have to go away . . . !" she wailed.

Blake eased into the closet and caught her up in his arms. He held her and hugged her and walked the floor with her while she cried. His shirt was soaked, but Sarah didn't seem to mind. She held on with all her might.

"I love you, baby girl," he whispered in her ear. "You'll never have to go away."

"But you fought!" Sarah said.

"Not the bad kind of fighting," Meredith said, smoothing the child's soft hair as she rested against Blake's wet shoulder. She smiled. "Sarah Jane, how would you like to have a brother or sister?"

Sarah stopped crying and her eyes widened. "A real live baby brother or sister?"

"A real live one," Meredith assured her. She looked up into Blake's soft, quiet eyes. "Because we're going to have one, aren't we, Blake?"

"Just as soon as we can," he agreed huskily, his eyes full of warmth and faint hunger.

"Oh, that would be so nice." Sarah sighed. "I could help you, Merry. We could make clothes for her. I can sew. I can make anything."

"Yes, darling," Meredith said with an indulgent smile.

"And Meredith isn't going anywhere," Blake added. "Neither are you, young lady." He chuckled as he put her down. "I can't do without my biggest helper. Who'll go out with me to feed the horses on weekends and help me talk to the men if you leave?"

Sarah nodded. "Yes, Daddy."

"And who'll help me eat the vanilla ice cream that Mrs. Jackson has in the freezer?" he added in a whisper.

Sarah's eyes brightened. "Vanilla?"

"That's right," he said. "Left over from your birthday party. Would you like some?"

"Blake, it's too late . . ." Meredith began.

"It is not," he said. "It's her birthday, and she can have more if she wants it."

"Thank you, Daddy." Sarah grinned.

"I guess birthdays do only come once a year," Meredith said, relenting. "I'll go and get it. And some cake."

"Amie will get it," Blake said, eyeing Meredith's clothes. "You and I have to change before we can join the party. We got soaked on your account, young lady," he told Sarah with a faint smile. "We thought you'd run out into the fields."

"Oh, I couldn't have done that, Daddy," Sarah said matter-of-factly. "I would have gotten my lovely party dress wet."

Blake laughed with pure delight. "I should have thought of that."

Mrs. Jackson had followed them upstairs and was sighing with relief. "Sarah, I'm so glad you're all right," she said, and smiled. "I was worried."

"You're nice, Mrs. Jackson," Sarah said.

"So are you, pet. Want to come and help me dish up some ice cream and cake while your mommy and daddy change clothes? And we could even make some cookies if you want to. It's not at all late. If your daddy doesn't mind," she added, glancing at Blake.

"Please, Daddy!" Sarah asked.

"All right," he said, relenting. "Go ahead. Your mommy and I will expect some when we get showered and changed. And they'd better be good," he added.

Sarah laughed. "Me and Mrs. Jackson will make lots," she promised. She took Mrs. Jackson's hand and went with her.

"We are a mess," Meredith said, looking down at her clothes.

"Speak for yourself," he returned. "I look great soaking wet."

She eyed him mischievously, her gaze running possessively over his hard muscles. "I'll drink to that."

He took her hand. "Well, come on. We'll get cleaned up together."

She went with him, expecting that he'd leave her at the door to the master bedroom, but he didn't. He pulled her into the bathroom with him and closed the door, locking it as an afterthought.

Meredith's heart went wild. "What are you doing?" she asked.

"We have to shower, don't we?" he said softly. His hands went to her blouse. "Don't panic," he whispered, bending to touch his mouth gently to hers. "We've seen each other before."

"Yes, but..."

"Hush, sweetheart," he breathed into her open mouth.

She was hungry for him. It had been so long. Too long. She gave a harsh moan, and the blood went to his head when he heard it.

"Do that again," he whispered roughly.

"Do...what?"

"Moan like that," he bit off against her mouth. "It drives me crazy!"

She felt his hands on her breasts when he pushed the blouse out of his way, and she did moan, not because he'd said to, but because the pleasure was so exquisite.

He reached out to turn on the shower and adjust the water, and then, his jaw set, his eyes glittering with desire, he stripped her and then himself and lifted her into the shower.

In between kisses, he soaped her and himself, and it was an adventure in exploration for Meredith, who'd never dreamed of touching and being touched so intimately. The soap made her skin like silk and the feel of his hands against her most secret places was unbearable delight.

He rinsed Meredith off, and himself, then turned off the water and reached for a towel. But he didn't dry them with it. Holding her eyes, he spread the towel on the tiles of the big bathroom floor, and catching her waist, he lifted her against him and kissed her with probing intimacy.

"We're going to make love. Here," he whispered, "on the floor."

She shuddered at the images that flashed through her mind. "Yes," she groaned, pressing hard against him so that her soft breasts flattened against the thick pelt of hair on his muscular chest.

He spread her trembling body on the thick towel and himself over her, his mouth demanding and slow, his body making the sweetest kind of contacts as he moved sensually over her.

She felt his hands on her and she shivered, but he kept on, evoking sensations she hadn't dreamed existed. She opened her eyes and looked at him and cried out, her nails digging into his shoulders as she lifted against his hand.

"I've never wanted you this badly," he whispered as he poised above her. "I don't want to hold back anything this time."

"Neither do I." She lifted her hands to his face. "I love you," she said, parting her lips as they brushed his with open sensuality. "I love you, Blake."

His hands contracted on her hips as he moved down, very slowly, his eyes holding hers so that he could see them while his body began to merge with hers. "I love you, too, honey," he whispered shakenly, jerking a little with each deepening movement. She started to lift up, but his hands held her still. "No," he murmured breathlessly, his eyes

still on hers. "No, don't . . . move. Don't rush it . . . God!"
His eyes closed suddenly and he shuddered.

She felt him, breathed him, tasted him. Her body shook
with what he was doing to it, with the exquisite slowness
of his movements, the depth . . . She clenched her teeth and
cried out in protest, her hips twisting helplessly.

"Blake . . . if you don't . . . hurry!" she wailed in anguish.

"Ride it out," he whispered at her ear. His body flowed
against hers like the tide, lazy and deliberate, despite the
sudden hot urgency that was burning them both. "It's
going to be good," he groaned. "Good . . . so good . . .
Meredith!" His body clenched. "Merry, now!"

She felt his control slip and she let go of her own, yielding totally, trusting him. And the tension all but tore her
to pieces before she felt the heat blinding her, burning her,
and she fell into it headfirst with tears streaming down her
cheeks.

His hands were in her hair, soothing her, smoothing the
wet strands away from her rosy cheeks. He was kissing her,
sipping the tears from her eyes, kissing away the faint sorrow, the fatigue, the trembling muscles.

She opened her eyes and his face came into focus. She
couldn't breathe properly. Her body felt as if it had fallen
from a great height. His eyes held hers, and there was adoration in them now, openly.

"The bed would have been better," he said, brushing her
mouth lazily with his. "But this was safer."

"She's making cookies," she told him wearily.

"She's unpredictable." He nuzzled her nose with his. "I
love you," he breathed, his eyes mirroring the statement.
"I couldn't admit it until today, but, oh, God, I feel it,
Meredith," he said huskily, his face taut with emotion that

made her heart jump with excitement. "I feel it when I look at you, when I'm with you. I didn't know what it was to love, but now I do."

"I've always felt that way about you," she whispered, smiling adoringly. "Since I was eighteen. Maybe even longer. You were the moon, and I wanted you so much."

"I wanted you, too. But I didn't understand why I wanted you so badly." He kissed her again. "You complete me," he breathed. "You make me whole."

Her arms linked around his neck, she buried her face in his throat. "I feel like that, too. Was it necessary to torture me to death?" She laughed shyly.

"It was good, though, wasn't it?" he said. "So intense that I thought I might pass out just at the last. I like losing control with you. I fly up into the sun and explode."

"Yes, so do I." She cuddled closer. "The floor is hard."

"The bed is unprotected."

She sighed. "Well, there's always tonight." She drew back a little. "Are you going to sleep with me?"

"No, I thought I'd sack out with one of the horses— oof!"

She withdrew her fist from his stomach. "Sarah Jane wants a brother or sister."

"At the rate we're going, that won't take long. There's nothing wrong with you," he added, emphasizing it. "And meanwhile, Sarah's going to have time to adjust to us and feel secure. Okay?"

"Okay. I'll stop worrying," she promised.

"Good. Now let's go get some ice cream," he said, moving away to get to his feet and pull her up with him. "I'm starving!"

She wanted to make a comment about men and their strange appetites, but she was too hungry to argue. Her eyes adored him. So much had come out of such a stormy, terrible night, she thought as he wrapped a towel around his lean hips and tossed an extra one to her. He loved her. He actually loved her. She smiled, tingling all over with the newness of hearing the words, of having the freedom to say them. It was like a dream come true. Or it would be, she thought, if she could ever give him a child. She had to force herself not to think about it. Anyway, Blake had said there was plenty of time.

Epilogue

Eight months later, little Carson Anthony Blake Donavan was born in Jack's Corner Hospital. Looking down at the small head with its thick crown of black hair, Meredith could have jumped for joy. A son, she thought, and so much like his father.

Sitting by her bed, Blake was quiet and fascinated as his first son gripped his thumb. He smiled down at the tiny child. "He's a miracle," he said softly. "Part of us. The best of us."

She smiled up at him tiredly and her hand touched the finger that was caught in the baby's grasp. "He's going to look like you," she said.

"I hope so, considering that he's a boy," he replied dryly.

She laughed. Her eyes made soft, slow love to his. "I'm so happy, Blake," she whispered. "He's the end of the rainbow. And I was so afraid that I couldn't give you a child."

"I knew you could," he said simply. "We love each other too much not to have a child together." He bent and kissed her soft mouth. "Sarah wanted to come, too. I explained that they wouldn't let her in here, but you're getting out tomorrow and she can see her brother all she wants to. She's coloring a pretty picture for him."

"She's been almost as excited as we have," Meredith said. "She'll love not being an only child. And it will give her some security. She still doesn't quite believe that she's safe and loved."

"It will take time," he said. "But she's coming around nicely."

"Yes." She smoothed her fingers lovingly over the baby's downy soft hair. "Isn't he just perfect, Blake?"

"Just perfect," he said, smiling. "Like his mother."

She searched his eyes. "No regrets?"

He shook his head. "Nobody ever loved me until you and Sarah Jane came along," he said quietly. "I can't quite get over it. I'm like Sarah—happiness takes some adjusting to. You've given me the world, Meredith."

"Only my heart, darling," she said softly. "But maybe it was enough."

He bent to kiss her again. "It was more than enough," he replied. The light in his eyes was so full of love for Meredith and his child that it was almost blinding. He smiled suddenly. "I meant to tell you—I met Elissa and Danielle in town just before I came here. They're bringing over a surprise for you." His eyes twinkled. "The store was a little crowded, full of people. I walked in, and do you know what Danielle said?"

Meredith smiled lazily. "No, what?"

"She pointed to me and said, 'Look, Mama, there's Sarah Jane's daddy!'" He grinned. "And do you know what, Merry? I think I'd rather be Daddy than president."

Meredith reached up and touched his mouth lovingly. "I'm sure Sarah Jane and little Carson will agree with that." She took his hand in hers and held it. "And so do I."

He looked down at his son, and foresaw long days ahead of playing baseball in the backyard and board games at the kitchen table. Of drying Sarah's tears and helping Meredith patch up Carson's cuts and bruises. Together, he and Meredith would raise their children and make memories to share in the autumn days. He brought Meredith's hand to his mouth and lifted his gaze to her quiet face. There, in her gray eyes, was the beginning and end of his whole world.

* * * * *

Keepsake

 Harlequin Books

You're never too young to enjoy romance. Harlequin for you . . . and Keepsake, young-adult romances, destined to win hearts, for your daughter.

Pick one up today and start your daughter on her journey into the wonderful world of romance.

Two new titles to choose from each month.

FOUR UNIQUE SERIES
FOR EVERY WOMAN YOU ARE...

Silhouette Romance

Love, at its most tender, provocative,
emotional... in stories that will make you laugh and
cry while bringing you the magic of falling in love.

6 titles per month

Silhouette Special Edition

Sophisticated, substantial and packed with
emotion, these powerful novels of life and love will
capture your imagination and steal your heart.

6 titles per month

Silhouette Desire

Open the door to romance and passion. Humorous,
emotional, compelling—yet always a believable
and sensuous story—Silhouette Desire never
fails to deliver on the promise of love.

6 titles per month

Silhouette Intimate Moments

Enter a world of excitement, of romance
heightened by suspense, adventure and the
passions every woman dreams of. Let us
sweep you away.

4 titles per month

Silhouette Desire •

1989
IS THE YEAR
OF THE MAN!

What makes a romance? A special man, of course, and Silhouette Desire celebrates that fact with *twelve* of them! From Mr. January to Mr. December, every month spotlights the Silhouette Desire hero—our **MAN OF THE MONTH.**

Sexy, macho, charming, irritating…irresistible! Nothing can stop these men from sweeping you away. Created by some of your favorite authors, each man is custom-made for pleasure—*reading* pleasure—so don't miss a single one.

Diana Palmer kicks off the new year, and you can look forward to magnificent men from **Joan Hohl, Jennifer Greene** and many, many more. So get out there and find your man!

Silhouette Desire's

MAN OF THE MONTH…

MAND-1